The Incident at Ingleton

Beau Monde Secrets, Book 3

Anne Rollins

ARE YOU SIGNED UP FOR DRAGONBLADE'S BLOG?

You'll get the latest news and information on exclusive giveaways, exclusive excerpts, coming releases, sales, free books, cover reveals and more.

Check out our complete list of authors, too!

No spam, no junk. That's a promise!

Sign Up Here

www.dragonbladepublishing.com

Dearest Reader;

Thank you for your support of a small press. At Dragonblade Publishing, we strive to bring you the highest quality Historical Romance from some of the best authors in the business. Without your support, there is no 'us', so we sincerely hope you adore these stories and find some new favorite authors along the way.

Happy Reading!

CEO, Dragonblade Publishing

Additional Dragonblade books by
Author Anne Rollins

Beau Monde Secrets Series
Secrets at Selwyn Castle (Book 1)
Discovery at Dogwood Cottage (Book 2)
The Incident at Ingleton (Book 3)

Chapter One

May 1818
Lancashire, England

After the noises, smells, and bustle of London, the vicarage in Ingleton seemed unnaturally quiet. At first, Lady Hester Bracknell found it difficult to sleep in the unfamiliar guest bedchamber. By the third day of her visit, though, she'd come to appreciate the peaceful setting. She particularly appreciated it when she woke up with a pounding headache, which was not by any means an uncommon experience, though certainly an unwanted one.

In the Bracknell family's London townhouse, it would have been hard to find a truly quiet place to rest during the worst of the pain. If there weren't callers visiting all afternoon, there would have been errands to run or calls to pay, and people would have been dashing in and out of the house all day. Hester's bedroom looked out into the street, which meant she heard carriages rattling along the road day and night.

Her bedroom in her older brother's parsonage, on the other hand, looked into the churchyard next to St. John the Baptist church. The long-buried dead made for quiet neighbors, and the shadow of a towering yew tree blocked much of the afternoon light from her window. Hester put a cold compress on her forehead, closed her eyes, and listened to the soft sounds of leaves rustling in the wind and distant birdsong. They were far more soothing than the bustle of Berkeley Square.

She had nearly fallen asleep before her sister-in-law, Rose, popped her head into the room. "Are you quite all right, Hester? Can I get you anything?"

Hester moved the compress off her forehead and opened her eyes, though the sudden brightness hurt. "It is only one of my bad headaches. If you have peppermint tea or willow bark, that might help. Otherwise, I will just try to sleep it off."

"I don't think we have either of those." Rose sounded genuinely regretful. "I do have some laudanum, though, left over from when Frank had a toothache. Would you like that?"

Hester sighed. "Only as a last resort. It can be dangerous, you know." She closed her eyes again and returned the cool cloth to her forehead.

Her brother ought to know the dangers of laudanum. They'd both watched it take control of Aunt Patience's life. Prescribed tincture of opium for her nerves, Aunt Patience took it daily, in greater and greater doses. If her supply ran out, she became restless, anxious, and sick to her stomach. Eventually, she died from accidentally taking too much laudanum.

At least, everyone said it was an accident. But how could they know for sure?

Hester refused to risk either the possibility of an overdose or of becoming dependent on the drug. The alternative methods of treating her megrims might be less effective, but they were also safer.

"Very well," Rose said. "I can send a maid to the apothecary for willow bark and peppermint. But if you need anything else, let me know."

I need my head to stop pounding! Hester kept that thought to herself, because there was nothing her sister-in-law could do to help. Sometimes a long afternoon nap put her megrims to rest. She had some hopes that the quiet coolness of her bedchamber might help sleep off the pain.

Unfortunately, sleep did not cure this headache. She woke up two hours later, her head still throbbing with pain. She blinked her eyes and looked around, so disoriented that she didn't even recognize the room. When she sat up, the abrupt movement made her stomach roil.

But as she looked around, she recognized the room. She was in the guest chamber of Frank's house, right where she should be. Someone—probably Rose—had placed a handbell next to the bed. Hester rang it, and though it took a few minutes, eventually one of the housemaids appeared.

"Yes, miss? I mean, yes, Lady Hester?" The young maid flushed at her error, then dropped a belated curtsy.

"I was wondering if I could have a cup of willow bark tea?" Hester whispered, because even the sound of her own voice hurt her ears.

"Yes, miss. I'll be back in two shakes of a lamb's tail."

How long, Hester wondered idly, did it take for a lamb to shake its tail? Certainly, nowhere near as long as it took to brew a cup of the apothecary's headache cure, which included peppermint, willow bark, and a hefty serving of sugar. Hester considered the bitter taste well worth the relief the remedy brought. Even willow bark tea could not entirely defeat one of her "sick headaches," but it pushed the pain back from a sharp throb to a dull ache.

Fortified by her drink, Hester forced herself downstairs to see if Rose needed help. She had been sent to Ingleton for the express purpose of helping her sister-in-law, since Rose's expected date of confinement was only a month and a half away. Much help Hester would be if she spent every afternoon cowering in her bedchamber!

Hester found Rose in the kitchen, helping the cook with dinner plans. Rose's golden curls had been confined to a severe-looking knot, and a long apron covered her morning gown. The apron protected Rose's clothing, but she had still acquired a dusting of flour across her nose, and her hands were buried deep in a mound of dough.

Hester's eyes widened at the sight of a lady in a delicate condition doing work that usually fell to servants. "Where did you learn how to cook?" she wondered aloud.

Rose's father, Lord Rufford, was a baron. Though the Rufford family was neither as wealthy nor as high in status as the Bracknells, Hester had assumed that Rose's upbringing must have been much like hers: a childhood spent in the nursery, followed by an education at the hands of an expensive governess, and concluded by a Court presentation to formally launch her into society. Though Hester had learned to embroider, net, and sew a hem, she'd never been taught the culinary arts.

Rose grinned at her. "Rather droll, isn't it? I've learned a lot from Mrs. Barnes." She nodded at the cook, who glanced up to return her smile before returning to basting a fowl. "I don't always help in the kitchen, but when we have guests dining with us, all hands are needed on deck!" She wiped her face, but succeeded only in spreading the flour smear.

"Ah, yes! Your dinner party!" Hester's heart dropped all the way to the floor. Somehow, she'd forgotten all about tonight's dinner, though Rose had been chattering about it since Hester's arrival.

"Of course, you don't have to dine with us if you don't feel well enough for company," Rose assured Hester. "We can send a tray up for you, if you prefer."

Hester very much preferred that option. When in good health, she enjoyed dinner parties as much as anyone. She liked meeting new people, because one never knew when one might make a new friend. But when she had one of her megrims, normally pleasant social interactions became a painful chore. She could not focus on conversations or remember new names when her head pounded the way it did today.

But it did not seem right to skip out on tonight's dinner. Hester knew this was the last dinner party that Frank and Rose would host for some time. Rose's *accoucheur*, Mr. Newman, advised all his patients to spend the last month of pregnancy resting. Rose and Frank, eager to do the right thing, intended to avoid most social events in the coming months.

"I don't want to miss this party. It will be the perfect chance to meet a few of your neighbors." Hester forced a smile, but the wrinkle on Rose's forehead suggested she remained unconvinced. "Can I do anything to help?" she offered.

By now, Hester had already realized that her training as an aristocrat's daughter hadn't prepared her to take on the work of managing a household. She wasn't sure how helpful she could really be during this visit. Still, she strove to be useful, so that some good would come of the scandal that drove her out of London for the rest of the season.

One of the maids, Daisy, showed Hester how to wash and dry dishes, and Hester took over the work in the scullery, leaving Daisy free to polish the silver. In a large country house, polishing silver would be the butler's job, but Rose and Frank did not employ a butler: only a cook, two maidservants, and a man-of-all-work.

Hester had just put the last teacup in the proper cupboard when someone knocked on the door. The upper housemaid, Hannah, scurried into the kitchen. "Mr. Butler is at the door, and he has a question for Lady Francis about the Lady's Aide Society. Where is she?"

"Lady Francis is dressing for dinner." Mrs. Barnes glanced at Hester. "P'rhaps you could keep Mr. Butler entertained until her ladyship comes down? Shouldn't be too long."

"Um." Hester quickly examined her morning gown, which had been thoroughly bespattered with water while she did the dishes. She shuddered to think what her hair looked like now. More importantly, she'd never met Mr. Butler. "Who is Mr. Butler?"

"The curate," Mrs. Barnes answered succinctly. "Lord Francis's assistant. He's new here, hired just a couple of months ago. I expect he's biding time 'til he gets a living of his own."

"I suppose I could go talk to him," Hester reluctantly agreed. It seemed highly irregular to converse with a gentleman to whom she'd not been properly introduced, but what else could she do?

She found Mr. Butler in the vicarage's lone sitting room, a comfortable parlor decorated in soft shades of blue and blush pink. Bookshelves lined one of the interior walls, and Mr. Butler stood before the shelves, perusing the titles. He turned around when Hester entered the room, greeting her with a smile and a bow.

"How do you do, Mr. Butler?" Hester returned his smile, but as she gradually took in all the details of his appearance, her heart sank.

After the disastrous conclusion of her entanglement with Simon Lowell, Hester had vowed to stay far away from handsome gentlemen with more fashion than fortune. She'd thought the task would be easy, that such men would be thin on the vine in a rural town like Ingleton. But Mr. Butler looked like precisely the sort of young man she needed to avoid!

The young curate wore gray pantaloons, tall boots, a white waistcoat, and a sedate navy-blue tailcoat. He had tied his cravat in the Mathematical style, and his hair fell in artfully arranged curls. As for the rest of him, he was what novel writers called "tall, dark, and handsome." He had coal-dark eyes, a straight nose, and a set of magnificent side whiskers.

"How d'you do, miss?" The young gentleman studied her for a moment, somehow giving the impression that he scanned her from head-to-toe without seeming the least bit forward or impudent. "I don't believe I've had the pleasure of being introduced to you?" The graceful arch of his eyebrows turned it into a question.

"I am Lord Francis's younger sister," Hester explained. "Hester Bracknell."

His face lit up with a bright, contagious smile. "Ah, Lady Hester! Yes, your brother told me you'd be visiting for a time. I hope you enjoy your stay in Ingleton. We are a friendly lot here, you know."

"I am glad to be here." That was a bare-faced lie. In reality, she felt miserable and wished she could hide in a darkened room again. Her headache had been temporarily subdued by the medicinal tea, but an ominous pulsation deep inside her head hinted that it was on its way back.

Hester did her best to chat politely with Mr. Butler, but it was nevertheless an enormous relief when Rose came down to speak to him. Hester made her excuses and hurried upstairs, wishing she'd taken Rose up on the offer of a dinner tray in her room. It might not be too late to change her mind, except that she did not want to cause trouble for Rose.

In just the few days since her arrival, she'd already seen how much harder Rose's advanced pregnancy made even such simple chores as helping to carry a basket of laundry or picking vegetables from the garden. Hester didn't dare add to Rose's work by requesting special treatment tonight. She would just have to bear with the pain as best she could.

Not wanting to overdress for a country dinner, she donned a simple white muslin gown. She reached into her jewelry box for her garnet heart pendant, then hesitated. Simon had given the necklace to her as a love-token. He'd led her out to a moonlit garden, clasped the golden chain around her neck, and kissed her. She'd gone to bed that night with a heart overflowing with joy, certain that a proposal would soon be forthcoming.

No, she could not wear that pendant *now*. Maybe never again.

Tears stung her eyes, but she held them back, knowing that crying would worsen her headache. Besides, she couldn't go down to dinner with reddened eyes or a tear-stained face. Everyone would see her distress, and wonder what was wrong. She couldn't allow that. No one in Ingleton was supposed to know about Simon or the scandal that had driven Hester out of London.

Hester firmly closed the drawer holding the pendant, wishing she could as easily close the door on all the mistakes of the past six months. Instead of the little red heart, she donned a necklace of coral beads. That would be ornament enough. She studied her reflection one last time, nodded, and forced herself up from her chair. Time to go play the part of a proper young lady.

Would Mr. Butler be dining with them tonight? She held her breath as she pondered that. Under other circumstances, she would have looked forward to further encounters with a handsome and personable young gentleman.

A village as small as Ingleton could offer little by way of entertainment, especially when compared to the season her mother and younger sister were still enjoying back in London. In a summer that stretched before her like an endless, dreary fog, the promise of a new acquaintance sparkled like sun-lit crystal.

But Hester resolved to turn her eyes away from the prospect. No more handsome young gentlemen! That way lay heartache, shame, and disgrace. The Bracknell family could not afford another smudge on the family name, which meant Hester could not afford even the most innocent of flirtations. On the whole, she rather hoped that Mr. Butler would not be dining at the vicarage tonight.

Chapter Two

W HEN WALTER HAWORTH arrived at Selwyn Castle, the butler led him directly to the green salon, which had been turned into a playroom for Lord and Lady Inglewhite's firstborn child, Viscount Elston. Everything breakable or valuable had been removed from the room, and mismatched rugs overlay the hardwood flooring, to prevent falls.

The room might look less elegant than when Walter last visited his cousin Ivy, but it also looked more homey. Maybe the toddler tooth-marks on the arm of the sofa contributed to that effect; certainly, the seashell pattern carved into the wood would never be the same again! The presence of Robbie himself, happily dragging a wheeled toy horse behind him as he trotted around the room's perimeter, might have been the biggest contributing factor to the sitting room's changed ambience.

While a nursemaid kept a careful watch on young Viscount Elston, the Countess of Inglewhite sat in the window seat, knitting. The late afternoon light glinted off Ivy's hair. Most of the Haworth cousins had some shade of blonde hair, from Rose Rufford's bright gold to Walter's own straw-colored locks. When the cousins played together as children, Ivy's warm brown eyes and auburn hair stood out from the rest of the family.

Back then, Walter had wondered why his cousin looked so different from the other Haworth descendants. After a particularly eventful Christmas party two years ago, it had become common knowledge that Ivy had inherited both her brown eyes and dark red hair from her now-deceased father, the fourth Marquis of Reading, Alistair Bracknell. Little Robbie had inherited the Bracknell red hair, too, though his hair was a shade lighter than his mother's.

Ivy put down her work and rose to her feet so she could greet Walter with a hug. Tall as he was, Walter had to stoop down to return the embrace.

"Your timing is perfect," his cousin informed him. "I am dining at the vicarage tonight, and you shall dine with me. I need not take the carriage if I have you to escort me."

"I shall?" Walter glanced down at his travel-worn clothing. He'd arrived by post chaise, so at least he had not spent all day crammed into a stagecoach, but he still felt grubby. "I could do with a bath and a shave first."

Ivy glanced at the mantel clock. "I doubt you have time for a bath, but I'll send a footman up to shave you. You'll do fine. There will only be a handful of people, anyway. The vicarage doesn't have a dining room big enough for large dinner parties."

Walter admitted defeat. "Very well. You can send someone up to shave me in, say, a quarter of an hour?" That would give himself time to find his shaving kit and wash up. He had no valet of his own, but he knew from his previous visits to the castle that the senior footman played the role capably.

Fortunately, Ivy also arranged for a maid to bring up a tea tray, so Walter restored himself with a strong cup of black tea. After a long day of travel, that made tonight's dinner seem a little less impossible. Walter had come to Ingleton to investigate a criminal suspect, not to socialize, but it would be churlish of him to avoid seeing Rose and Frank, given the opportunity. Rose was his cousin, too, though he saw her less often since her marriage took her to Lancashire.

The walk from the castle to the vicarage also refreshed him. A delicious breeze flirted with the spring-green leaves in the park.

Unfortunately, gusts of wind also threatened to ruin Walter's hair, which the overzealous footman had enthusiastically curled, brushed, and arranged *a la Brutus*.

Walter, never having desired to play the dandy, thought his stylishly-disarrayed hair looked ridiculous. This might be the style favored by young men under the influence of Lord Byron, but whoever heard of a blond Byron?

"I look like a fop," he grumbled aloud.

"Nonsense! You look very dashing tonight," Ivy assured him. "I shall be proud to show my cousin off to our neighbors."

Walter snorted and shook his head, but he held his tongue. He'd rather not get into a quarrel with his cousin about whether or not he looked dashing. He hadn't wanted any of this—not the evening clothes, the *coiffure*, or the dinner party itself. He did it only for Ivy's sake. He felt grateful that she'd agreed to put him up for the duration of his investigation.

Last year, some person or persons unknown had falsified the account books at the Haworth Home for Orphans, embezzling money by inflating the reported costs of such necessities as coal, candles, food, and fabric, then pocketing the difference. The theft amounted to no more than a hundred pounds, but that still made the crime a hanging offense.

Walter, having been trained as a solicitor, handled all the legal matters associated with the orphanage his grandfather had founded. Much to his dismay, this meant that some members of the Advisory Board overseeing the orphanage had suspected *him* of stealing the money! The board had dragged him in for a meeting to discuss the matter one sunny afternoon in April. While birds sang and flowers bloomed, Walter had to defend himself.

"Why would I bother falsifying the expense accounts only to steal such a small sum of money?" he'd demanded. "A hundred pounds is a fraction of my annual income." Because Walter would someday inherit his father's landed estate, Grandfather Haworth hadn't bequeathed him a large fortune like what the other grandchildren received, but Walter possessed a competence of his own. He had no need to steal!

Whoever had doctored the orphanage's ledgers had done it very carefully, pocketing small amounts over the course of nearly a year and a half. It must have taken a great deal of meticulous planning. Walter couldn't imagine wasting so much time for so small a reward.

"You could have gambling debts!" the most suspicious of the board members had suggested. He squinted at Walter through narrowed eyes, looking like a cat ready to pounce the moment its prey twitched.

Before Walter could defend himself, his uncle had intervened on his behalf. "If you can produce a single witness who has ever seen Walter gambling, I'll pay *you* a hundred pounds, Mr. Yorke." Lord Rufford slanted an amused look towards Walter. "I've heard stories of philanthropists with double lives, but so far, no one has produced the slightest evidence that Walter has anything to hide."

"It's not that we think you likely to steal. It's only that you're one of the few people with the opportunity," a less ireful board member had pointed out.

Walter had left that meeting determined to clear his own name by finding the real criminal. He and his brother-in-law, the new chaplain at the orphanage, had worked out a plan for their investigation. So far as they could tell, only a handful of people ever recorded expenses in those ledgers. One suspect, the previous matron of the orphanage, had died back in November. Another suspect, the former chaplain of the orphanage, had left to take a position as curate in Ingleton. Walter had traveled to Lancashire to investigate the curate. Walter wanted to ask Neville Butler a few questions, and he preferred to ask them face to face, so he could watch Butler's expression as he answered. It was far too easy to lie in writing. With any luck, though, he'd get a chance to talk to the curate tomorrow, and he might be on his way back to Bristol before the week ended. Walter even harbored a secret hope that the curate might be one of the guests at dinner that night.

Unfortunately, that was not the case. The vicarage at Ingleton was a handsome brick building that had weathered nearly a century, but it could not be described as spacious. Ivy had not exaggerated when she told Walter that the dinner party would be small.

Walter and Ivy were led through a small, wood-paneled foyer into the front parlor. This room, decorated in a pretty striped wallpaper, was suitable for entertaining a family, or a group of gossiping Lady's Aide members, but it could not have contained the dozen or more guests commonly found at large social functions.

In addition to Walter and Ivy, the guests consisted of Mr. and Mrs. Anderson of Greyfriar's Hall, and Lord Francis's sister, Lady Hester Bracknell. The Andersons seemed to be polite, good-natured people. Mr. Anderson was tall and lanky; Mrs. Anderson was pretty and plump. Both of them smiled a good deal, and neither of them seemed any more memorable than other country gentry Walter had met.

Lady Hester was a different story. Knowing she was Lord Francis's younger sister and Ivy's cousin, Walter had unthinkingly assumed that Lady Hester, like them, would have red hair and perhaps a smattering of freckles.

But Lady Hester looked nothing like what Walter had imagined. She was tall for a woman, standing only a few inches shorter than Walter himself. Her eyes were a darker shade of brown than Ivy's, her pale skin was unmarked by freckles, and her hair was a rich chestnut brown. She had high cheekbones, a sharp chin, and a widow's peak. She looked nothing like her cousins, so far as he could tell.

Instead, Lady Hester looked beautiful, elegant, and as removed from her humble surroundings as the bright evening star. Walter caught himself gazing at her far longer than courtesy allowed. Gradually, he realized that the expression on her face, far from being friendly, welcoming, or even interested, was one of languid disinterest. She had neither Lord Francis's lively good humor nor Ivy's warmth. He politely turned his eyes away.

I am probably not genteel enough for her company, Walter concluded. Not that it mattered, of course. He was not particularly interested in hobnobbing with the aristocracy. He made an exception for Ivy, Rose, and their husbands, but in general, he had no desire to infiltrate *tonnish* social circles. Frankly, he had more important things to do.

When the butler announced dinner, Walter offered to escort Mrs. Anderson into the dining room, leaving Lady Hester behind. Let her sit next to her brother, who presumably was of sufficiently elevated status to meet her standards! Walter was perfectly willing to enjoy himself chatting with other guests. Why should he mind being snubbed by a spoiled aristocrat?

He tried to put Lady Hester out of his mind entirely as the company entered the dining room. This chamber looked to have been recently re-papered in a rose-colored floral pattern, and a handsome mahogany dining set dominated the room. But again, Ivy had not exaggerated when she called the room small. The heavy rectangular table was really only long enough to seat six diners. In order to accommodate Walter, an extra chair had been squeezed in at one corner.

Walter snagged that chair before his hosts could tell him where to sit. He suspected that Lord Francis would have taken that awkward corner seat if Walter hadn't grabbed it first, and that wouldn't be fair. As an uninvited guest, Walter ought not inconvenience anyone else. Rose glared at Walter before she sat down next to him at the foot of the table, but she wisely refrained from asking him to move.

But Rose got her way in one regard: she placed Lady Hester on Walter's other side. According to formal dining etiquette, this meant Walter should divide his attention between the two neighbors, speaking to both ladies equally.

Chatting with Rose was easy enough, since they had family

gossip to share. Rose told Walter about the life of a clergyman's wife, and Walter told her about his work at the Haworth Home. He said nothing about the criminal case that brought him to Ingleton, but he talked about the new matron, Miss Miller, and about how his brother-in-law, Ernest Robinson, was adjusting to his new position as chaplain of the orphanage.

As for Lady Hester, he tried to talk with her. He really did. But she answered him with monosyllables and never suggested any topic of conversation on her own. When he asked about her journey, she said only that it was "tolerable." When he asked how she liked Ingleton, she offered a smile and a shrug. "I've only seen a little of it," she said, and went to taking slow sips of her water. Seeming supremely uninterested in anything to do with Walter, she asked no questions of him.

Lady Hester? More like Lady Frostbite! Walter thought. Clearly, she did not wish to converse with him.

He finally left Lady Hester alone to eat in silence. Strangely, though, she only picked at her food. Probably she was used to *haute cuisine* rather than plain English cooking. With every passing moment, Walter's opinion of her sank further. How could she be so supercilious when her older brother was warm and outgoing?

Walter amused himself for some time by thinking up implausible explanations for the differences between Lady Hester and Lord Francis. Perhaps they had been raised in separate households: he by a loving mother, she by a frigid, parsimonious aunt. Maybe she was not Frank's sister by blood at all, but a foundling left on the doorstep of—where was it that the Bracknell family lived? He could not remember.

Walter turned to the silent, pale-faced girl beside him. "Where do you reside when you are not in London, my lady?"

She looked up from the tart on her dessert plate, startled. "Bracknell Hall, usually, along the Severn River. Or sometimes Trescott Abbey, near Eastbourne."

"I've been to Eastbourne." Had they finally found a viable

conversation topic now that the meal was almost over? "When I was a boy, we had a picnic on Beachy Head. Rather a frightening place."

"Frightening?" Lady Hester's eyes widened. "But it's lovely! You get such a splendid view of the channel from the cliffs."

"And a splendid drop if you fall off the cliffs." Walter shivered. He remembered that childhood picnic mostly because he'd been terrified of heights. He and Eugenia, his older sister, kept several yards between themselves and the edge of the cliff at all times, but only their strict governess had prevented his younger sister, Freddy, from standing with her toes at the very brink.

Lady Hester wrinkled her nose. She managed to look dainty and elegant even while showing disgust, which seemed profoundly unfair. Nasty thoughts ought to lead to a nasty appearance, oughtn't they?

"That is hardly a reasonable fear," Lady Hester argued. "As long as one has wisdom enough to stay away from the edge, one need not worry about it." She put a tiny bite of dessert in her mouth, then followed it up with a dainty sip of water.

Walter struggled to control the frown tugging at his face. "Sometimes people worry about things even when they know there is no real danger. When I was a child, I was very afraid of the dark, even though I knew there was nothing in the nursery that could harm me." He spoke as calmly and evenly as he could, not wanting to reveal how strongly he disagreed with her.

Childhood fears were no laughing matter to him. He still remembered the panic of waking up in the night, certain that a ghost or boggart hid inside the large chest of drawers at the foot of his bed. If he called for help, his nurse would come with a candle. She'd open up each drawer to show him that the chest contained nothing more ominous than breeches and stockings. Walter would agree with her and promise to go to sleep. But the moment the nurse left the room, he once again felt as if something in a dark corner of the room watched him with hungry eyes.

Lady Hester shrugged. "Oh, well, children may be afraid of anything. But surely most people leave those fears behind in childhood. I cannot imagine being afraid of the dark *now*."

The dismissal in her voice stung Walter to the quick, and his hand tightened around his fork. He silently counted down from five before responding.

"I must beg to differ, ma'am. In my experience, a case of bad nerves can strike a person of any age." Walter thought of his nervous Aunt Edith and the anxieties she felt any time her children traveled far from home. Then he thought of stock characters from novels and the trouble they caused their fictional families. "Especially wealthy people with too much time on their hands who fancy themselves ill in order to make their lives more interesting."

He'd thought Lady Hester's complexion was already as pale as pale could be, but her face turned a shade whiter. A tremor shook her hand, and she lowered her fork. *Confound it!* She'd taken his words personally, hadn't she? He'd offended her while she was a guest in her own brother's household. That was badly done.

Walter hastened to apologize. "I beg your pardon, Lady Hester! I intended no offense, I merely meant—you know, in novels. . ." He closed his lips tightly, realizing it probably wouldn't help to claim he'd only been thinking of characters like Mr. Woodhouse from *Emma*. Real life was not the same as fiction.

"I was not offended, Mr. Haworth. I hope I never give anyone reason to think me a nervous, discontented woman." Lady Hester's voice once again sounded disinterested and reserved, and she refused to look Walter in the eyes.

Maybe that prompted Rose to rise from her seat, signaling that the ladies should withdraw. Ivy looked surprised, probably because she hadn't finished the biscuits on her plate. But unless Walter mistook himself, Lady Hester looked relieved as she swept out of the room, bound for the parlor.

He would have to make a better apology. Hopefully, he could

find a quiet moment to speak to her when the gentlemen rejoined the ladies for tea and coffee.

Walter never got the chance to apologize, though. When the gentlemen returned to the parlor, Lady Hester had vanished. Walter discreetly asked Rose about her absence and learned that she'd retired to her room with a "sick headache."

Or, more likely, hurt feelings, Walter concluded. He felt ashamed of himself. She might have behaved superciliously to him, but he'd had no desire to insult her. Meeting her again was going to be awkward now. He could only hope that the business of interviewing Neville Butler would be wrapped up quickly, so he could escape Ingleton before he inadvertently offended Lady Hester again.

Chapter Three

WHEN SHE REACHED her guestroom, Hester's first instinct was to ring for her maid. But of course, she did not have her lady's maid here. At home, she shared a lady's maid with her younger sister. Since Julia had stayed in London for the rest of the season, the maid had naturally stayed with her. Here in the vicarage, the upper housemaid served as lady's maid when necessary, though Hester had gathered the impression that Rose often dressed and undressed herself.

Or maybe Frank undressed Rose, a wicked thought whispered. Hester shoved the intimate image out of her mind as quickly as possible. She did *not* want to contemplate the private details of her brother's marriage. Ugh! Bad enough that everyone knew they were having a baby.

One of the housemaids had filled the ewer on the dressing table with fresh water. After she washed her face, Hester dampened a face flannel, then lay down in bed and covered her forehead with the wet compress. It only helped a little, and she lay awake for an eternity while her head pounded and her thoughts spun around in circles.

In hindsight, Hester realized she ought to have excused herself from tonight's dinner party. Her sick headaches left her in no fit state for entertainments, even small country dinners. But Frank had been eager to introduce her to Lady Inglewhite, who apparently was their late uncle Alistair's only child, born on the wrong side of the blanket. This made Lady Inglewhite Hester's and Frank's cousin by blood, if not by law.

Hester hated to disappoint her brother, the more so as she knew Frank and Rose were both worried that she would find life in the country dull. And it was true that Hester worried that she'd be bored living in a tiny town, with no visits to the opera, garden parties, or routs to keep her entertained. But she also felt relieved to be far from London. Far from handsome cavalry officers whose gambling debts forced them to marry an heiress, or gossiping tabbies who influenced everyone's guest lists. Far from Mama's disappointment or Julia's astonishment at Hester's behavior.

Frank and Rose must know why Hester had been exiled to Lancashire, but they hadn't said a word about the scandal. Initially, Hester appreciated their tact, but now she wondered if it would have been better to sit down and explain everything, so they'd know her side of the story. She could have explained about Simon: the love-tokens, the secret letters, the kisses and caresses they'd shared behind closed doors when they met at parties. That might have been better than them knowing only the disgrace of Hester having been caught kissing a married man in a dark corner of the Duke of Creighton's garden.

As it was, she had no idea what Mama had told Frank and Rose when she made arrangements for Hester to visit them. According to Mama, Hester was here to look after her sister-in-law as her confinement drew near. When Hester wrote her apologies to her friends in London, she'd cited her frequent megrims as a reason for leaving town in the middle of the season. Surely country air and simple, farm-fresh food would be better for her health than smoke and fussy gourmet cuisine.

So she'd hoped. But she was confined to bed with another sick headache. Worse, she had the vague sense that she'd somehow managed to offend Mr. Haworth. Because he was Rose's cousin, he was in some sense part of Hester's extended family. (Was there such a thing as a cousin-in-law?) She hadn't wanted to insult him at all, but it was hard to act the part of a witty conversationalist when she was in agony.

That was what other people seemed not to understand about her headaches. When wealthy young ladies claimed to "have the headache," everyone tacitly understood that such headaches provided an excuse for avoiding unwanted social encounters. When Hester told people she was subject to frequent headaches, they assumed she meant no more than that. No doubt Mr. Haworth thought so, too; it would explain his criticism of valetudinarianism.

Hester's headaches were no mere excuse. They disrupted her life, thwarted her plans, and forced her to spend hours resting when she'd rather be living the way other people did. After the incident with Simon, she'd resolved to behave with circumspection, so that she would be a credit to the Bracknell name rather than a disgrace. Unfortunately, it was hard to make a good impression while experiencing disabling pain.

As she lay in bed trying to ignore the pulsating agony in her skull, Hester lost track of time. She had no idea how long she'd been lying in the dark before Rose gently tapped at the door.

"Are you quite all right, Hester? Can I get you anything?"

"If you could send up another cup of that medicinal tea, that might help," Hester suggested. The apothecary in Rocheford St. Peters, the nearest market town, sold a "headache" blend that used willow bark as the base and peppermint for flavor. It worked about as well as most treatments did.

"Very well," Rose said. "I'll have Hannah bring you another cup of that tea. And if you need anything else, let me know."

I need my head to stop pounding! Hester kept that thought to herself, because there was little her sister-in-law could do to help. The combination of her headache tea and a good night's sleep might help. Sometimes she went to bed in agony and woke up in the morning free of pain.

Unfortunately, this megrim was not so easy to shake. She woke up the next morning with a dull ache in her head, promising more pain if she moved around too much, ate the wrong thing, or ventured out into the bright sunshine. Instead of taking country walks or helping Rose in the garden—physical exertions that would only make a megrim worse—Hester spent most of the day in the parlor with all the curtains drawn.

The day after that, however, Hester woke up to find her pain gone and her appetite fully returned. Just in the nick of time, too, because Lady Inglewhite had family visiting the castle, and she invited the residents of the vicarage to come up and spend an afternoon with them. Frank excused himself on account of a vestry meeting, but Rose and Hester took advantage of the offer to use the luxurious Inglewhite carriage.

In truth, Hester would rather have skipped this visit. She found it difficult to keep straight the names of the two young Inglewhite girls, daughters of the previous earl. The elder was a girl in her teens who looked to be fast approaching the end of her time in the schoolroom. Hester understood why a girl so close to adulthood to be allowed to socialize with the adults, but the younger Selwyn daughter could not have been more than nine or ten. Hester was surprised to see her allowed to take tea with her mother, her aunt, and the guests from the vicarage.

Stranger yet, the young heir to the Inglewhite title was allowed to roam loose about the room, making jabbering sounds that were almost, but not quite, words. Little Lord Elston toddled up to Hester and handed her a half-eaten biscuit. She stared at it, baffled. She had no idea what etiquette called for in such a situation, so she thanked the child and placed the soggy biscuit on the nearest table.

"I'm sorry if he's bothering you!" Lady Inglewhite swooped in with a handkerchief and quickly scrubbed Lord Elston's grubby hands.

"Is there no nursery in the castle?" Hester watched Lady Inglewhite's face fall, and immediately realized she'd said the wrong thing. "I mean no criticism," she clarified. "I'm just not used to seeing young children playing with the family."

"You must blame the Haworth side of my family for that." Lady Inglewhite sounded a bit sheepish. No doubt she knew how unusual this approach to parenting was among the aristocracy. "My grandparents liked to have children about the place, rather than confining them to the nursery. That is how Uncle and Aunt Rufford raised us too, isn't it?" She smiled at Rose.

Rose pulled a face. "What they may have done when you were young, I know not," she told her cousin. "But I very clearly remember being allowed to sit in Mama's boudoir and watch her dressing for dinner parties or balls. And I know we rambled all over the manor in our games." She turned to Hester and smiled. "Papa must have been unusually tolerant towards children, because I even remember playing in his study while he signed letters."

"Oh, I remember more than that," Lady Inglewhite put in. "I distinctly recall you spilling ink all over his correspondence. On more than one occasion, I might add."

Rose giggled. "I am sure he sometimes regretted his leniency, but I loved being able to spend so much time playing by his side."

"Oh, I see." Hester blinked, not at all sure how to respond. "How charming!"

She supposed it *was* charming in a way, but it was so vastly different from how she had been reared! At Bracknell Hall, the children stayed in the nursery or schoolroom until they were old enough to display good company manners. Growing up, she'd spent far more time with her nursemaid and her governess than with her mother. As for Papa, he used to spend every Parliamentary session in London, so she had sometimes gone months without seeing him.

But of course, that much was true of Lord Inglewhite's family as well, since he also held a seat in the House of Lords. "You must miss Lord Inglewhite," Hester said to Lady Inglewhite. "I am sure it is hard to stay behind when he is in London."

Lady Inglewhite's smile wilted. "Yes, I do miss him. I do not think it is good for Robbie to be apart from his father so long. But

Richard and I both agreed that London is no place for so young a child, and—" she hesitated, then blushed. "The truth is, I am in the family way again, and I would not like having to navigate another London season at a time when I might often be indisposed."

"Yes," Rose agreed, "those early months are so exhausting." She flicked her eyes towards Hester and smiled wryly. "But we are probably boring you with all our child-rearing talk. I promised Phoebe that we'd play hide-and-seek. Would you like to join us, Hester?"

"Ah. . . of course, I'd be delighted." Hester glanced at Lord Elston, who was happily pushing a wooden horse back and forth over the carpet. "Can a child that young play hide-and-seek?" she wondered aloud.

"Not very well," Lady Inglewhite said. "But in any case, I'm afraid it's time for his n-a-p. Say good-bye to our guests, Robbie!"

"Bye!" Robbie yelled over his shoulder as he ran towards the waiting nursemaid. His mother followed in order to scoop him up, kiss his cheek, and hand him to the nursemaid, who carried him away.

So, Lady Inglewhite did sometimes let her servants care for the children. But surely other parents in the *ton* did not spend so much time with their children. Did they? For the first time, Hester realized she had little idea how other families lived in the privacy of their own homes. For all she knew, her family might be the exception rather than the rule.

She resolved to ask Frank about it when she got the chance. He'd traveled more widely than she had, and as a clergyman, he moved in a wider range of social circles. He probably knew better than she did what was and wasn't the norm in *tonnish* households.

For now, though, she set aside the question to play hide-and-seek with the Selwyn girls. At first, she felt self-conscious, afraid it demeaned her to play like a child. But soon, she became caught up in the challenge of the game. Hide-and-seek was much easier to play on familiar territory. If she'd been in Bracknell Hall, on the second story, she would've known all the good places to hide. Selwyn Castle, being almost entirely new to her, presented a greater challenge.

Before everyone scattered to find hiding places, Lady Inglewhite (the current countess, not the dowager) insisted on a few rules. Only the ground floor and the first story were fair game; the second story and the attics were off limits, as was any room in which servants were working.

"No hiding in the kitchen or the servant's hall," Lady Inglewhite explained. "I don't want you getting in anyone's way. And no trying to open locked doors."

"We wouldn't do that!" the older Selwyn girl insisted. She turned to her sister. "Isn't that right, Phoebe?"

Hester bit back a laugh when she saw the younger sister hide her hand behind her back and cross her fingers. For a moment, she wondered if she had a duty to warn Lady Inglewhite that at least one of the children did not intend to follow the rules.

No, she decided. That wouldn't be sporting. Besides, how likely was it that a child of ten knew how to pick a lock, anyway? It seemed an unlikely talent for the daughter of an earl to have picked up.

Rose and the younger Lady Inglewhite played too, though the dowager retired to her own chamber to rest. Hester was relieved not to be the only adult involved in the game. If nothing else, it should give her some competition. Lady Inglewhite probably knew the castle better than anyone else.

For the first round, Phoebe was the seeker. While she closed her eyes and counted, the other players scattered. From the banging and crashing of doors, Hester guessed that the older Selwyn girl planned to hide in a room on this floor rather than the ground floor.

Lady Inglewhite slipped away through a narrow wooden door that blended in with the paneled corridor walls. Curious, Hester peered through the open doorway and saw a servant's staircase. Wasn't that breaking the rules, though? They weren't supposed to enter any rooms where servants were working! On the other hand, this was Lady Inglewhite's home. The servants would not be surprised if the countess appeared in the offices.

Hester thought Lady Inglewhite had the right idea in heading to the ground floor, but since she had no desire to get lost in the castle's back hallways, she took the main staircase instead of the servant's stair. She slipped through the first doorway she passed and found herself in the library. It was a handsome, well-appointed room, with wooden settles framing the fireplace, walls lined with bookcases, and—window seats! Perfect!

Hester sat in the nearest window seat and pulled the drapes shut. She tucked her legs underneath her and leaned against the glass of the bow window, smirking to herself. It would be a long time before anyone found her here!

To her dismay, the door opened, and footsteps clipped against the hardwood floor. Then the door swung shut. Someone else was in the room, but those were not a child's footsteps. They sounded much too heavy. Who was in here with her?

Chapter Four

WALTER CAST A quick look around the library, though it was clear he'd beaten Ivy to the room. He was alone, without even the crackle of a fire to disrupt the hush. According to Ivy, Lord Inglewhite used this room as his office when in residence. With him away, the large wooden desk was bare of papers, documents, or books. Maybe that was why the emptiness of the room felt so oppressive.

Feeling too restless to sit down while he waited, Walter paced back and forth in front of the empty hearth. When the door swung softly open, he turned around. Tension he hadn't even noticed seeped out of his neck and shoulders when he saw it was only Ivy.

"Thank you for being willing to speak to me." He did not whisper, but he kept his voice low, not wanting anyone walking past the library to overhear.

"What is all this about?" Ivy frowned as she tucked a loose strand of hair back behind her ear. "You've been quite vague about what brought you to Ingleton."

"Yes, and I don't know that I can be any clearer now," Walter admitted. "All I have are questions and suspicions, not evidence. And it's only a matter of shillings and pounds. Not the end of the world either way. There may be no need for anyone outside the board to ever know about the crime."

Unless, of course, the money had been embezzled by some-one alive and well and intent on committing further crimes. As much as Walter wished the home could just brush the matter under the rug and forget about it, he worried that other charitable organizations or businesses would suffer if the board simply ignored the theft.

"But what makes you suspect—" Before Ivy could say more, the sound of galloping feet made them both look towards the door. "The children are playing hide-and-seek today," Ivy explained. "I'm supposed to be playing with them."

"I won't keep you from your game," Walter promised. "But since I am here and can speak unreservedly for a moment, I'd like to ask you to keep your eyes and ears open to anyone talking about philanthropy or charitable organizations. Let me know if you hear anything suspicious, will you?"

"Of course." Ivy frowned. "But why does the board suspect—"

He interrupted her, wanting to be precise in his wording. "*Suspect* may be too strong a word. Let's just say the board is asking questions about who pilfered the money, and why."

"I should think the *why* would be obvious," Ivy pointed out. "Doesn't everyone need money?"

Walter shrugged. "I suppose so, but embezzling so little money hardly seems worth it. Unless we have an enemy. Someone with other motives for the theft, I mean." He couldn't imagine who might bear a grudge against the Haworth Home for Orphans, but he also couldn't afford to overlook that possibility.

Ivy raised her eyebrows. Walter needed no words to interpret the skepticism on her face. But before she could elaborate further, Lady Phoebe poked her head into the room.

"Aunt Ivy! I found you!" she said triumphantly. She stared at Walter, blinking. "Who are you?"

"This is my cousin, Mr. Haworth," Ivy explained. "He's visit-ing us for a while, because his physician recommended he take a country holiday."

It certainly sounded plausible, except that if Walter wanted nothing more than time in the country, he could have gone to Northcote Manor, which was much closer to Bristol. Spending a few weeks at Northcote would have made his father happy, too.

"And I wanted to be on hand in case Rose—Lady Francis, I mean—needed any help during her confinement," he added. That ought to be explanation enough.

Ivy snickered and sent Walter a speaking glance. "Much help a young bachelor would be! What do you know about pregnancy or childbirth?" She said it affectionately, though. "Why don't you come play hide-and-seek with us?"

"Um." He couldn't remember the last time he'd played hide-and-seek with anyone. He saw his sister's son occasionally, but little Ned was only just old enough to begin playing games more complicated than Peek-a-Boo.

"Please, Mr. Haworth?" Lady Phoebe clasped her hands together in petition. "There are ever so many hiding places on the first story!"

In the face of such enthusiasm, what could he do but agree? "Very well."

Walter followed Ivy out the room, but before the door closed shut behind him, he heard a faint rustle. He glanced back over his shoulder and saw the drapery move, as if someone or something were sitting behind it.

He turned half-way around and stared at the curtain, wondering if one of the children had been hiding in the room. Rather an unpleasant prospect, that. But the drapery remained motionless, and he could hear nothing louder than his own breathing. Maybe a draft in the room had moved the curtain.

What did it matter, anyway? Neither he nor Ivy had said anything the least bit incriminating. He'd spoken as vaguely as possible, precisely because he had no idea whether they'd be interrupted. So far as he remembered, neither of them had mentioned Neville Butler by name.

"Are you coming, Walter?" Ivy poked her head back through the open door.

"Oh, yes. Very sorry. I was woolgathering." He let the door click shut behind him and followed his cousin back to the first story so he could join in the next round of hide-and-seek.

WALTER DISCOVERED THAT Neville Butler was surprisingly hard to pin down. The curate had been out of town when Walter arrived, and when he returned, he seemed to run from one corner of the parish to another on various errands. Since his brother-in-law was a clergyman, Walter thought he knew something about clerical life. Apparently, he was mistaken. When Neville Butler and Frank Bracknell talked about their parish duties, Walter could understand only half of it, at best.

Walter had been at the castle for a week before Butler finally found time in his busy schedule to meet with him. Even then, the curate showed up nearly a quarter of an hour late. He arrived at the castle flushed and grimy, mopping sweat from his brow.

"Terribly sorry about the delay." Butler smiled apologetically. "I was visiting a shut-in and I could not for the life of me get her to stop talking. I suppose it's understandable when one gets few visitors, but..." He shrugged as he took the seat Walter indicated.

They met in the library, since the room was not in use. There were, of course, many rooms in the castle that would have done just as well, but Walter thought the business-like setting best fit the nature of this conversation.

"You're probably wondering why I wanted to talk to you," he began.

But Mr. Butler grinned at him. "Since you're a Haworth, and I used to be the chaplain at the Haworth Home for Orphans, I'm going to assume this has something to do with that institution. Am I right?"

"Yes, in a manner of speaking." Walter drew a clean handkerchief out of his pocket, took off his spectacles, and began to clean the lenses. They were not in the least bit smudged, but he'd learned this trick as a legal clerk. Cleaning his glasses provided an excuse to evade someone else's gaze, which made it easier for Walter to conceal any reactions he didn't want to reveal. Of course, it also prevented him from studying Butler's expression, but he was willing to accept that trade-off.

"The board had some questions about who handled the management of the home last year," he explained. "We know the matron, Mrs. Fairfax, had been ill off and on for some time. Did someone else step in to manage things?"

Butler rubbed his chin, looking thoughtful. "Well, that depends on which things you mean. I believe the housekeeper and the teachers took on some of the children's care when Mrs. Fairfax was indisposed. Other duties probably were neglected to some extent."

Walter lifted his chin, replaced his spectacles, and nodded. "That makes sense." It also matched what the housekeeper and the instructors reported. "Did the housekeeper handle the paperwork, too? For example, keeping track of expenditures?"

A line formed between the curate's brows. "Not usually. Some of it I handled for Mrs. Fairfax. Some of it Miss Eversley handled—she's the senior teacher, you know. Or was during my time."

"Ah, yes. She holds the same position now." It hadn't occurred to Walter to talk to Miss Eversley, because he had been under the impression that the teaching staff had nothing to do with the financial management of the home. He'd have to remedy that as soon as he could or ask Ernest to talk to Miss Eversley for him.

Butler's admission that he'd sometimes handled the expenditures seemed far more important. "Did you ever help balance the account books?" Walter asked the question as casually as possible, but he kept his eyes fixed on the curate's face.

Butler frowned and looked off to the side, as if trying to remember. "Balance them? No. But I did sometimes record expenditures. Normally, Mrs. Fairfax managed the ledgers, but her eyesight weakened in the last years of her life, so she often had someone else do it. I believe you'll find that the housekeeper, Mrs. Johnson, also kept track of purchases."

This, too, matched what Walter had already heard. "Was there anyone else who handled the ledgers? Or had access to them?"

"Had access to them?" Butler raised his eyebrows. "The office door was rarely locked, so anyone could have looked at them. It's possible that Miss Eversley helped with them; I don't know that for certain. I believe Mrs. Johnson usually kept the accounts during Mrs. Fairfax's illness, though." He frowned. "Why do you ask?"

Walter listened intently. Butler's voice sounded steady, un-flustered. Walter detected neither anxiety nor anger in his tone. But the way the curate played with the buttons on his jacket could hint at nervousness. And Walter noticed that Butler kept glancing away from him, rather than making steady eye contact.

"We're just trying to get things back in proper order at the home," Walter lied. "All the paperwork in the office seems to have been left at sixes and sevens. Of course, the children were always well-cared for, even when Mrs. Fairfax was indisposed."

"I should hope so!" Butler sounded genuinely dismayed. "I can assure you, I saw no indication that any of the orphans were neglected or ill-treated. No matter how sick the matron was, someone made sure they were looked after."

Walter nodded. "Good to know. I suppose matters did not slip so much after all."

"Have you any more questions, Mr. Haworth? I've no more meetings today, so I am quite at your disposal." Butler looked him in the eyes and smiled angelically.

"No more questions." Walter returned the smile as benevolently as possible. "If I do think of anything, I'll be in touch."

He did still have questions, but he could scarcely ask Butler outright if he had embezzled money from the orphanage. Naturally, the former chaplain would deny that. In confirming that Butler had the opportunity to doctor the books, Walter had achieved his objective. For now, at least.

"Please do let me know if there is any way I can help. I know that Mrs. Fairfax's death was a great loss to the home. But I hope the new matron is working out?" Butler's rising voice made a question of it.

Walter nodded. "I believe she struggled a bit at the beginning, but she's found her footing quite well by now." That was an understatement, since the new matron had, in fact, been the one who noticed the discrepancies in the old ledgers. If not for Miss Miller's attention to the orphanage's finances, no one would ever have noticed the crime.

For a moment, Walter wished the pilfering had gone undetected. Would it really do any good to know that money had been taken, if the board couldn't definitively prove who took it? On the whole, he might rather not have known. And he certainly would rather not have been called in front of the board and grilled about the theft! He'd been fortunate in having two of the board members on his side, but he hadn't known that going into the meeting.

"Well, if you ever do need my help, you have only to ask. Haworth Home is near and dear to me." Butler smiled, but his eyes looked surprisingly cold. "If that is all?"

"Yes, yes, you may be on your way," Walter told him. "I'll be staying here at the castle for the next few weeks, so if I do think of anything, I'll be sure to ask."

Butler's eyes widened for a brief second. Then he collected himself. He smiled again, though this smile, like the last one, did not reach his eyes. "I'm sure I'll see you around, then. Good-day, sir."

The moment he left the room, Walter pulled out his notebook and began jotting down details of the conversation. He had no particular talent for sniffing out a lie or reading people's hidden intentions, but some of Butler's reactions seemed odd. He seemed almost dismayed to hear that Walter would be lingering in the area. And that was very interesting indeed.

Walter tucked his notebook back into his pocket and took a quick glance around the room, making sure he hadn't disturbed anything or left anything behind.

He noticed that this time, the drapes in front of the windows had all been tied back, letting bright spring sunlight into the room. If that was how they were usually left, why had the curtains been pulled shut over the window seat the last time Walter was in the room?

Maybe there really had been an eavesdropper. Strange that whoever-it-was hadn't revealed themselves as soon as they realized they were overhearing a private conversation. Strange, and potentially troubling. Once again, Walter felt relieved that neither he nor Ivy had discussed any explicit details of his investigation. No one listening in would have the faintest clue what they were talking about. He hoped it stayed that way.

Chapter Five

YOUNG MR. HAWORTH must be up to something, Hester concluded. But what? She had only overheard bits and snatches of his private conversation with Lady Inglewhite, but she'd heard enough to speculate that something criminal was afoot.

She couldn't imagine, though, why Lady Inglewhite would have anything to do with the crime. A wealthy countess could have no reason to steal—not unless she'd somehow run up gambling debts. Such things did happen; something similar had happened to Hester's older brother, Lord Crowthorne, who resorted to stealing jewelry at a house party in an attempt to pay off his debts. In theory, Lady Inglewhite could have a secret like that.

But Hester felt certain there must be a better explanation. For one thing, she might very well have misunderstood what little she'd heard. She had not, after all, heard either Mr. Haworth or the countess reveal an intention to commit crimes. Nor had the conversation constituted a confession of past crimes.

Hester knew only that Lady Inglewhite and her cousin shared some secret connected to theft and—if she'd heard correctly—to philanthropy. Philanthropies, she knew, were often managed by a clergyman, or connected to religious organizations. What if Frank was somehow involved in this situation? Or was about to be dragged into it? After Crowthorne's theft and Hester's scandalous public kiss, Frank could not afford to be involved in anything the least bit dodgy. Probably he had nothing to do with the case, but Hester resolved to keep an eye open and ear out for any scraps of information related to the matter, just in case.

Since Mr. Haworth was Rose's cousin, as well as Lady Inglewhite's, Hester had plenty of opportunities to observe him over the next week. He chatted with Rose after church on Sunday morning, dropped in to visit on Monday afternoon, and dined at the vicarage on Wednesday.

Though Hester kept a wary eye on Mr. Haworth, she didn't hear him say anything in the least bit incriminating, or even particularly interesting. His conversation tended to focus on the current news from London and Manchester, and on events in the lives of his extended family. Occasionally he discussed recent advances in natural history or medicine, but that seemed to be his only interest outside his work.

The Haworth family had made their fortune through West Indian trade, so Hester assumed Mr. Walter Haworth helped run the family business. Naturally, he couldn't discuss something as crude as trade or finances in mixed company, so she had very little idea of what work he did. Something to do with refining or selling sugar, probably—wasn't that the sort of thing merchants in Bristol did?

Neville Butler, Frank's curate, also paid frequent calls at the vicarage. Unlike Mr. Haworth, Mr. Butler improved upon further acquaintance. On Tuesday, he and Hester had a pleasant conversation about poetry and their favorite poets.

Mr. Butler avowed himself a fan of Percy Shelley and Lord Byron. Hester, on the other hand, preferred the work of Maria Grammar, an obscure poetess from Cumberland. Mr. Butler had never even heard of her work, but that was no surprise. No one Hester met ever seemed to have heard of Grammar's first book of poems, *The Waters of Dreaming*. Mr. Butler promised to keep an eye out for any of Maria Grammar's poems, which was more than most people were willing to do.

On Friday, Mr. Haworth was invited to take tea and play cards after dinner. Rose and Frank teamed up together and thoroughly trounced Hester and Mr. Haworth at a game of whist. Rose celebrated their victory with a smothered yawn, then suggested an early end to the evening.

"It really wasn't fair," Mr. Haworth argued. "Since you two are married, you had an advantage in reading each other's faces. My partner and I don't know each other well enough to read each other's signs." He caught Hester's eye and shrugged his shoulders. She smiled wryly in commiseration.

"Table talk is a form of cheating," Frank reminded him. "I hope you are not suggesting that I, a devout son of the Church, cheated at cards?" He arched his eyebrows.

"It wouldn't even be worthwhile to cheat, since we're playing for counters rather than coins." Rose gathered up the counters to return to their box, while Frank shuffled the cards.

Mr. Haworth snorted. "And a good thing, too! It's never wise to gamble with your relatives. A sore loser might hold a grudge and ruin every family party for decades."

Rose laughed. "Maybe in other families, but not in ours." She turned her smile towards Hester and invited her into the conversation. "Does your family play whist, Lady Hester? Or do you prefer other games?"

Hester frowned. She couldn't remember the last time she'd played a game of any sort with her siblings. "My father does not like us to gamble." She clamped her mouth shut afterward, hoping no one would ask why.

It had been decades since the current Marquis of Reading lost a fortune on the tables, but there were plenty of people who might still remember his youthful excesses. His gambling might not have been as legendary as his raking, but it was bad enough. Hester did not want to remind anyone of the Bracknell family's disgraceful past. Sufficient unto the day were the scandals thereof, she reasoned.

"A very wise position," Mr. Haworth said. "People have lost whole fortunes to the tables."

"Yes," Hester said softly. "I know." She looked across the table at Frank, wondering if he felt as uncomfortable with the topic as she did. But he was occupied with putting the cards neatly in their box, and showed no awareness that the conversation might have wandered onto thin ice.

"I have *never* understood people who spend thousands of pounds on card games or dice," Rose said. "If I were going to waste a fortune, I would spend it on hats and jewels."

Frank chuckled, but he also reached across the table to take hold of her hand. "The wife of a country clergyman probably has few chances to show off Parisian fashions or flashy gemstones. Ingleton is not even big enough to have assembly rooms of its own."

"It's true." Rose scrunched up her face, but a giggle belied the expression of distaste. "I suppose I might show off the latest modes when we dine at the castle, but it hardly seems worth impressing Richard and Ivy. I don't believe Richard would even notice whether a gown was new or ten years old."

Frank grinned. "No, fashion is not Inglewhite's strong suit," he agreed. "Ivy might notice what you wear, but I doubt she would judge anyone negatively for wearing fashions that are passe."

Mr. Haworth jumped back into the conversation. "My sister, Freddy, is married to the chaplain at an orphanage, and she sometimes grumbles about the way clergymen's wives are supposed to dress in accordance with their rank while simultaneously being so spiritual and unworldly that they are above caring for fashion and furbelows."

"What could be wrong with fashion?" Hester stared at him, puzzled. Women were supposed to dress fashionably in order to show off their family's wealth and their own good taste. According to Mama, dressing appropriately for a given social occasion was an important skill.

A smile teased at the corners of Mr. Haworth's mouth. "Nothing is wrong with fashion, unless people spend money on it that should have been spent on something else."

She thought at first that Mr. Haworth was mocking her, but his voice sounded too kind for that. She wondered what, exactly, he meant by money that "should have been spent on something else." Maybe he had in mind people who skimped on wages for their staff in order to pay the dressmaker's bills.

"And I suppose the same is true of most luxuries," Frank put in. "Eating French cuisine when one's tenants are starving is bad form. Or it ought to be."

Hester's mouth gaped open. "When did you get so serious, Frank? I remember when you spent hours learning to tie a cravat just to impress—"

Frank held up his hand to stop her and chuckled. "Please, Hetty, don't tell Rose those stories! The Haworths are rather serious people, you know. They will not understand our ways."

Our ways, meaning the Bracknell family? Or our ways, meaning the *ton*? Hester could not tell which he meant. Either way, her brother had provided her with a new way to tease him. For the first time that evening, a genuine smile broke across Hester's face.

"Very well, Frank. I won't tell them how many hours you spent searching for the perfect cologne at Truefitt & Hill." He had taken her with him to run errands that day, promising her an ice at Gunter's when they were done. She very clearly remembered waiting hungrily for him to find the perfect cologne. Perhaps it hadn't literally taken hours, but every minute seemed like an eternity to a girl who just wanted an ice.

A flush of red rose on Frank's cheekbones. "That was back before I was ordained! I was still rather frivolous then."

"He still wears Spanish Leather." Rose covered one side of her mouth as she spoke, as if whispering a secret.

"There's nothing wrong with wanting to smell pleasant." Frank's blush had faded, but he kept his gaze fixed on the card table. "Don't we owe it to our neighbors not to stink?"

"I have never cared for cologne myself," said Mr. Haworth. "The scents seem too strong to me, even when people use only a dab. And when someone wears too much perfume or cologne, it feels like a punch in the nose." He wrinkled his nose and shuddered theatrically.

"Yes, strong scents give me a headache," Hester admitted. "I prefer lavender water or rose water." Those fragrances were more subtle, and they didn't linger for as long. "I suspect many of the people who wear too much scent really need to make better use of their soap. Scented soap bothers me much less than cologne."

"Scented soaps are rather beyond most people's pocketbooks. But maybe advances in manufacturing will make them less expensive." Mr. Haworth rose to his feet and pushed his chair back.

"Leaving so soon?" A yawn undercut Rose's protest.

"I need sleep," Mr. Haworth said, "and so do you, I suspect. But you'll be dining up at the castle next week, will you not?"

"We will," Frank agreed. "I'll be interested in hearing the news from London. Ingleton may know things that aren't yet in the papers."

This was news to Hester, who hadn't heard about the dinner invitation, but she had no objection to dining at the castle. Her interest in the upcoming dinner party only grew when she learned that Mr. Butler would be attending, too. He'd been so busy with his work over the last couple of days that she hadn't had a chance to chat with him.

That changed the day before the dinner party, when she ran into the curate outside the church. Hester had brought a book and a blanket outside, so she could sit in the shade of the enormous yew tree that graced one corner of the churchyard.

Hester had been looking at the book in her hand instead of where she was going, and she would have crashed into the young curate if he had not caught hold of her arm to stop her. His touch startled her with all the force of a gunshot.

"Lady Hester! Are you quite all right?" he asked anxiously.

She looked up and blinked, surprised to find him standing so close to her. "I am fine." She glanced down at her arm, still in his grip. She could not decide whether to be grateful to him for protecting her from accident, or indignant because of the liberty he'd taken.

He released her at once, and stepped back to give her space. "My apologies! I did not want you to get hurt."

"Thank you." Hester stood awkwardly in place for a moment, not sure what to say in this situation. "I hope you are doing well?"

Mr. Butler smiled broadly, revealing a dimple at the corner of his mouth. "I am doing quite well, thank you." His eyes drifted down to the cloth-bound book Hester clutched to her chest. "Is that another collection of Miss Grammar's poems?"

"No, I don't have a copy of her most recent book. It came out after I'd already left London for the country. I suppose there might be a bookseller somewhere hereabouts that could order it for me."

"Ah, that's a shame. I shall have to keep my eyes open for it."

"That would be very kind of you." But also, rather pointless. Frank said there was a good bookseller in Lancaster, but Hester doubted it would carry the work of such an obscure poetess.

She nodded politely and began to move past Mr. Butler. To her surprise, he turned on his heel and walked beside her all the way to the shade of the yew tree. As they wended their way past grave markers stained by time or leaning at a tilt, she snuck a quick glance up at Mr. Butler's face. He wore a pleasant expression, but she could read no hint of what he was thinking.

"Have you ever taken gravestone rubbings, Lady Hester?"

Hester cocked her head. "I don't know what you mean, Mr. Butler." Of all the things he might have said to her, she had not expected that.

"I had a friend in college whose hobby was collecting tombstone rubbings," he explained. "He used a large piece of paper and some artist's charcoal." Mr. Butler stopped beside a small, upright tombstone to demonstrate. "He'd hold the paper against the surface of the stone, then rub charcoal over it. A record of the engraving would be left on paper. He framed some of the finest ones and hung them on his wall."

"Interesting." Hester drew her brows down as she studied the moss-covered lettering on the stone. "But it seems a rather morbid thing to hang on your walls."

"I suppose it is different if the tombstone belongs to your ancestor," Mr. Butler suggested. "Or if you have some other local connection. But at least if people take rubbings of the tomb-stones, there is a record on paper, should the stone later break or be lost."

How did a gravestone get *lost*? Hester wondered. Before she could ask, Mr. Butler continued talking.

"Anyway, if you were to look at the birth and death dates on all these grave markers, you'd see that many of the deceased were young children."

"Isn't that always the case? Young children are so fragile." Hester herself had lost two siblings. One had been stillborn before her own birth, and the other died of croup at only two months old. Hester still remembered the second loss, including the way her mother retreated from the rest of the family to mourn in silence. It had been a dark time in the household.

"Indeed." Mr. Butler's face fell into solemn lines. "That's precisely why I'm interested in the Havisham Hospital plan. I don't know if you've heard of it?"

"Noooo." Hester felt as wary as a doe scenting an approaching wolf pack. Mr. Butler was about to try peddling something, though she could not have said how she knew that.

"Sir Henry Skelton of Havisham Hall originated the plan," Mr. Butler explained. "He was inspired by the *Hôpital des Enfants Malades* in Paris. He thought England ought to have a children's hospital, too. But naturally, founding a new institution requires a great deal of work and a great deal of money, so I have been tasked with soliciting—"

Much to Hester's relief, an unfamiliar man poked his head out of a side door and called: "Butler! We're all waiting!"

Thankfully, Mr. Butler stopped in the middle of his fundraising speech. "Ah, my apologies. I have an appointment with some of the vestry members. We shall have to pick up this conversation later." He bowed to her, then hurried towards the church.

Hester felt strangely relieved to watch him walk away. She'd been right about him trying to sell her something. He undoubtedly wanted money for this new hospital, or infirmary, or whatever he called it. He must have assumed that because Hester's father was a marquis, she could afford to help support the charity.

Well, the more fool him! Hester had only a modest allowance for clothing, accessories, and other sundries. If he were hoping for a generous donor to endow the new charity, he was barking up the wrong tree.

More disappointing yet was the fear that he'd accosted her and conversed with her only because he wanted to collect money for the hospital. She'd assumed that his walking with her through the churchyard meant he enjoyed her company, that he wanted to spend time with her. Now it seemed he only wanted to hear the clink of a coin in the alms box.

Well, no great loss! It wasn't as if she'd fallen in love with Mr. Butler. It was only a minor disappointment. She resolved to take the disappointment as a reminder that she needed to avoid romantic entanglements. The best way to avoid further damaging her reputation would be to ignore all the handsome young men around her, even if they did have dimples. Or spectacles. Not that she knew any handsome *gentlemen* with spectacles, of course, since Mr. Haworth was in trade.

Her heart jumped when she saw the owner of the spectacles approaching, ducking his head as he stepped underneath a low-hanging branch. He touched his hat in greeting, smiling uncertainly.

"Good afternoon, Mr. Haworth." Hester reluctantly closed

her book. "What brings you to the churchyard?"

He cast his eyes about the churchyard, and his smile took on a distinctly rueful turn. "I don't suppose you'd believe me if I said I came here to visit someone?"

Hester blinked in surprise. Was that. . . a joke? She didn't think she'd ever heard serious Mr. Haworth crack a joke. Perhaps he was a little more human, a little less solemn, than he'd originally seemed.

"What I like about the churchyard is how quiet all the neighbors are." He gestured towards the gravestones surrounding them. "It's a place where you can hear yourself think."

The corners of Hester's lips curled up in a slight smile. "That's why I came out here to read," she explained. "It's a quiet, shady place, where I won't be interrupted."

His smile wavered before flickering out. "In that case, I apologize for interrupting you."

He bowed, then turned and stepped away before she realized that he thought she'd been referring to his interruption. Oh no! She hadn't meant to snub him. She opened her mouth, intending to call him back, but then thought better of it. She had, after all, come out here in the hopes of enjoying a good book and a lovely spring day. And what did she have to say to Mr. Haworth, anyway?

She picked up her book and stared at the page, trying to focus on Thomas Gray's melancholy verse. Suitable though the elegy was to her current surroundings, she could not follow a single line. She and Walter Haworth could have nothing in common with each other, which was just as well. She had vowed to avoid all romantic entanglements, hadn't she? Avoiding one attractive, eligible gentleman would be difficult enough. It would have been even trickier if Mr. Butler had a rival.

~~Just as well, really.~~

Chapter Six

WHEN HE ARRIVED at Selwyn Castle, Walter's plan was simple. He intended to interview Neville Butler, decide whether the curate warranted further investigation, and if not, go back home. He'd imagined that he'd be in and out of Ingleton in less than a week.

More than a fortnight later, if someone asked Walter why he lingered near Ingleton, he would be hard-pressed to explain himself. At best, he would have said that he enjoyed spending time with relatives whom he rarely saw in person. Once Lord Inglewhite wrote home to announce that he planned to play hooky from Parliament in order to visit his family, Walter had an excuse to further delay his return to Bristol. No one would think it at all odd if Walter stayed at the castle a little longer so he could see Ivy's husband.

But of course, that was not the whole truth. Fond as Walter might be of his cousins, he would rather have been ensconced in his own bachelor quarters, handling his usual work. By now he must be far behind on all his correspondence. In truth, Walter's relatives alone wouldn't have normally kept him in Lancashire this long. He stayed primarily because of his concerns about Neville Butler.

A single throwaway comment from Frank had revealed that Butler was assisting a wealthy landowner who wanted to set up an infirmary specifically for young children. Sir Henry Skelton might be right that the English people needed a hospital for children. Young children and infants were particularly vulnerable, often being the first to fall when an epidemic hit, or when crop failures caused widespread hunger. Walter had no opposition to the proposed charitable institution.

However, Neville Butler's involvement in the plan troubled Walter. On the face of it, the curate's interest in the hospital made sense, too. As Walter knew very well, Butler had experience working with charitable organizations. After Butler's time as chaplain of the Haworth Home, he might very well be looking for a similar position at another institution.

Or he might be looking for a new organization he could defraud.

Was Butler a saint in the making, or a particularly nasty sinner, willing to steal from some of the most vulnerable members of society? Until he could answer that question with a reasonable degree of certainty, Walter didn't feel comfortable giving up his investigation.

In the meantime, Walter wrote to Ernest, letting him know Butler's account of who at the home might have handled the ledgers. In Walter's opinion, the next step involved taking a closer look at the handwriting in the ledger, to see how many people really had recorded expenditures. If all the falsified entries were written in the same hand, that might provide a clue to the thief's identity. If, on the other hand, more than one person recorded falsified expenditures, that would complicate matters.

That wasn't something Walter could do himself. The board members were unlikely to let Walter handle the ledgers, given that at least some of them had suspected him of being the thief. Ernest Robinson, on the other hand, had not come to the home until after the thefts ended. The board would probably trust him with the accounts, just as Walter trusted him with the details of his investigation. For now, Walter could only wait for Ernest to report on his findings.

If Walter had a third reason for extending his visit at Selwyn Castle, he did not like to admit it, even to himself. It might be the case that when he passed Lady Hester on a walk into town, his eyes lingered longer on her tall, elegant figure than on anyone else. He might, hypothetically, invent reasons to drop in at the vicarage in the hopes of catching a glimpse of her. He hadn't had a great change of heart about her personality; she still seemed proudly aloof in all her interactions. But something about her face, her voice, and her graceful movements drew his attention time and time again.

He admired her as a man might admire any attractive woman, that was all. He didn't *fancy* her, though. Nor did he expect anything to come of his admiration. Even so, he hid his fascination with Lady Hester from his Ingleton cousins. It was entirely too ridiculous to be admitted out loud, and it most certainly could not be written in a letter. He could only hope that such a foolish infatuation withered as quickly as it had blossomed, leaving him in peace.

When the Earl of Inglewhite returned home to see his family, the countess hosted a dinner party for some of the local gentry. Walter dined with them, of course, as did the entire party from the vicarage. As they gathered in the drawing room before dinner, Rose announced that she intended to spend most of the evening reclining on a sofa.

"My ankles are so swollen I can't even fit into my half-boots!" Rose grumbled to Ivy.

Walter slipped out of the conversation and scurried to the other side of the room, certain that he didn't want to listen while his female cousins discussed pregnancy symptoms. They probably would prefer privacy for this conversation.

The corner to which Walter fled was, unfortunately, occupied by Lady Hester Bracknell and Neville Butler. They sat deep in a conversation, heads inclined towards each other. They both flinched like startled deer when they saw Walter approaching.

"Very sorry to disturb you." Walter glanced back over his

shoulder, wondering if he ought to find a different corner of the room to hide in. "I ought not interrupt your tête-à-tête."

Lady Hester wrinkled her nose, as if she smelled something nasty. "Nonsense," she said coolly. "We were only discussing the poetry of Maria Grammar. I suppose you are not familiar with it?"

"Indeed not," Walter confessed. "I don't read much poetry." Or any poetry. Of course he'd had to read classical poetry in his schooldays, but he remembered little of it. He'd been far more interested in learning about Galen and Hippocrates.

Mr. Butler and Lady Hester exchanged a speaking glance. Walter suspected they were appalled by his lack of culture. The tips of his ears burned with shame.

"I prefer books of information," Walter said apologetically. "I'm afraid the most recent thing I read was an article about Dr. Lannec's invention for more clearly hearing heartbeats."

"Oh?" Lady Hester's delicate eyebrows lifted with what looked like interest. That was encouragement enough to set Walter chattering.

"You've probably seen physicians listen to a patient's heartbeat by resting their head on the patient's chest, haven't you?" he asked.

"I suppose so." A doubtful line formed between her dark, graceful eyebrows.

"I certainly have," Mr. Butler said. "It's not useful only for hearing heartbeats, though. It's also a good way to listen for pneumonia."

"Yes, precisely! And Dr. Lannec's invention allows physicians to hear a patient's lungs or heart much more clearly, without having to directly touch the patient. It's a hollow wooden tube that carries sound, much like an ear trumpet, I suppose. Though I have never studied acoustics in any depth." He did not want to be mistaken for an expert on sound. He'd only explored acoustics in an attempt to understand Lannec's invention.

"Goodness, Mr. Haworth, you ought to have to been a physician yourself." The corners of Lady Hester's mouth quirked up almost imperceptibly. Had he not seen the way the corners of her eyes crinkled, Walter would have thought her faint smile was false.

Walter drew in a deep breath. "I did have some aspirations after the field of medicine when I was younger, but those were only childhood castles-in-the-air."

"What did you study, then?" Butler asked.

"Law." The corners of his mouth tugged down in an automatic frown. "A worthy field of study in itself, of course." His father had insisted that reading law would be far more useful to the family, and his grandfather had reinforced the suggestion with promises of an ample allowance while Walter studied under a solicitor.

"But not, perhaps, the field you were most interested in?" For once, Lady Hester's dark eyes looked soft and sympathetic.

He shrugged and glanced away. "My legal training enables me to be of use managing the charities my grandfather established. I may not treat the ailments of the world with physic, but I help provide conditions in which abandoned children can grow healthier and stronger."

At least in theory. In practice, even the best food and most comfortable housing could not protect a child from all the world's ills. Especially not if the child came to the home malnourished to begin with. And that was nothing compared to the suffering of the many hundreds of children not lucky enough to be found and cared for. Not all of the world's orphans could be saved.

Walter flicked his eyes over to Mr. Butler, once again wondering if the young curate could possibly be evil enough to steal money from an orphanage. Could he use this conversation to test his theory? He might not get a better chance.

"Of course," Walter said cautiously, "it takes a good deal of money to do such work. Whole fortunes could be spent caring for the suffering in England, and that would be only a drop in the bucket. With so much need, even the loss of a single penny might have unfortunate consequences." He held his breath as he waited to see how Butler would respond.

But Butler nodded, his face looking suitably grave. "It is truly the Lord's work, and I feel privileged to have been involved in it, even in a small way." He smiled at Lady Hester. "I don't know if I told you, but I served as the chaplain at the orphanage founded by the late Frederic Haworth. He must have been a great man to have spent so much of his fortune on the poor, and it is fortunate that his family continues to carry out his mission." The curate's smile turned obsequious as he shifted his gaze from Lady Hester back to Walter.

Flattery will get you nowhere, Walter thought crossly. But he found nothing to fault in Butler's response. Maybe Butler really was the virtuous young clergyman he seemed. Maybe Walter ought to go back to the home and take a second look at the papers left behind by the previous matron. She would have had more opportunities to falsify the records, anyway. Under normal circumstances, the home's chaplain would have nothing to do with buying food or fuel.

Walter toyed with the idea of returning to Bristol, until a scrap of conversation overheard after dinner convinced him that he needed to stay in Ingleton. Once the women had withdrawn to the drawing room, the men poured second (or third) glasses of wine, leaned back in their chairs, and began to discuss politics, sport, and the sort of gossip considered too racy for genteel ladies.

With Frank on one side and Lord Inglewhite on the other, Walter felt more relaxed than at most dinner parties. Despite whatever dandyish tendencies he might have had when he was young, Frank was sincerely committed to the good of his parish. Lord Inglewhite had also been a clergyman before inheriting his title. Neither of the two men at all fit the stereotype of the dissipated aristocrat.

Instead of pretending to be interested in the latest boxing match or amused by risqué humor, Walter could instead engage in a perfectly rational conversation about the ancient practice of rush-bearing, which had died out in most parts of the country but was still practiced in Lancashire. From there it was an easy step to discussing other curious traditions found in rural villages.

During a lull in the conversation, scraps of other people's talk filtered into Walter's awareness. Mr. Anderson asked Lord Inglewhite a question about the number of lambs born on the home farm this spring. Frank, who pastured sheep on the parish's glebe land, jumped into the conversation.

Walter, being supremely uninterested in animal husbandry, turned to listen to the conversation across the table. Mr. Butler and an unfamiliar young man had their heads together, laughing at something.

"—of course, it would be rather awkward if the girl were an absolute antidote," the young stranger said. "A man wants to find a little pleasure in the marriage bed, doesn't he?"

"Oh, I don't know," Butler replied. "A hefty dowry and good family connections go a long way towards making a man comfortable." Both men chuckled. "Take that Bracknell girl, now. Her portion may only be modest, but the Marquis of Reading controls three different livings. A clergyman who married into that family would be assured of a good benefice."

"Oh, is that the way the wind blows?" the stranger asked. "I wondered what appeal that whey-faced chit held for you."

"The appeal of a steady income," Butler agreed. "Not that her dowry would hurt, mind you." He glanced across the table, caught Walter's eye, and raised his eyebrows. "Are you on the hunt for a wife too, Haworth?"

"Not particularly. I've no desire to set up a nursery yet." Walter turned away, pretending he found their conversation boring rather than in poor taste. He took a sip of port and schooled his face to hide his disgust.

He wondered whether he ought to warn Lady Hester about Butler's intentions. The daughter of a marquis probably wouldn't encourage the suit of a curate who lacked valuable social connections, but Walter didn't like to think about Butler preying on innocent young women.

Or did Butler's remark bother Walter only because his prey was *this* particular young woman—the girl Walter admired? Walter drained the last of his wine and told himself not to be such a fool. He could think of half-a-dozen young ladies in Bristol more beautiful, more suitable, and more amiable than Lady Hester.

When the men finally joined the women in the drawing room, Walter kept an eye on Lady Hester. She sat next to Rose, not even bothering to look up at the men who'd just entered the room. Walter relaxed and went to speak to Ivy.

But the next time he looked back at Lady Hester, Butler had taken a seat near her. He must have said something witty, because both women started laughing. A spurt of anger made Walter grit his teeth and clench his hands, but even he didn't know whether he was angry on Lady Hester's behalf, or on his own.

Heaven knew Walter had no cause for jealousy, but still. . . it didn't seem fair that Butler was so much more successful at flirtation than Walter had ever been. Such socializing did not come easily to him. When Walter spoke with men from his grandfather's sphere of life, he knew what to say and what not to say. He could discuss the latest parliamentary reports or the price of corn, the rates of illegitimate children or the work of the West African Squadron.

But he could not talk to women about politics or business, since those subjects were considered inappropriate for mixed company. Talking to a lady from the aristocracy raised an entire host of new issues on top of that. Her life must be very different from his.

A voice interrupted his unhappy cogitations. "Walter, what are you thinking about? You look miserable!"

Walter looked his cousin Ivy in the eyes, twisting his mouth into a wry grin. "I was just wondering what on earth a man like me would have to say to the daughter of a marquis."

She raised her eyebrows. "You've never had any trouble talking to *me*," she pointed out.

He gaped at her for a second. "I didn't think of you, because you're my cousin." But Ivy was the natural daughter of a marquis, and she'd been raised alongside Rose in Lord Rufford's household. She was part of the aristocracy by birth, rearing, and marriage.—And she was right that Walter never had trouble conversing with her.

Walter simultaneously adjusted his glasses and some of his notions. Then a smile spread across his face. "Thank you, Ivy. You've been immensely helpful." At the very least, she'd given him a little more confidence.

Chapter Seven

THE MONTH OF May ended with a week of golden sunshine, burgeoning gardens, and untimely summer heat. All the windows in the vicarage were propped open to let in any hint of a breeze. Poor Rose gave up on housework entirely. She spent entire afternoons lying on the sofa with her feet propped up, lazily fanning herself to keep from being overheated. Even this was a compromise, though: her doctor wanted her to keep to her bed, since her due date was only a few weeks away.

Eager to help the relatives who had taken her in after her disgrace, Hester tried to take over Rose's usual work about the house. Managing even so small a home as the vicarage proved to be much more challenging than she expected. Normally, Rose directed the servants and lent a hand when necessary. Now that was Hester's job.

Hester quickly realized that she was not an adequate substitute for her sister-in-law. Having been raised in a wealthy household, she'd never learned her way around a kitchen, never made a bed, and had no idea how to launder anything. Rose gave her instructions, and the servants responded kindly to Hester's efforts, but the experience was humbling, to say the least.

Fortunately, the early heat wave did not last. The first of June brought a change in the weather. Dark clouds rolled in, the temperature dropped, and the wind picked up.

"We're going to have rain before the day is over," Frank predicted. "I'd better bring my umbrella."

"You're still going out? When it looks like that?" Hester gestured at the wind-driven clouds skating across the sky. It looked to her like the rainstorm was moving in quickly.

Frank shrugged. "Needs must when the devil drives. Mrs. Whitney will be expecting me, and I promised to bring a book so her granddaughter can read to her."

"Don't they have books of their own?" Hester protested.

Her brother raised his eyebrows. "Probably not, actually. They don't exactly have extra pounds sitting around."

Feeling abashed, Hester hung her head. "Of course. I should have realized." Not once in her life had she needed to calculate the cost of a book at Hatchard's or the Temple of the Muses. She simply ordered what she wanted and had the cost added to her family's account. Once again, she'd forgotten how different most other people's lives were.

"Ingleton is too small to have its own circulating library," Frank explained. "Although I believe Lady Inglewhite is trying to get one established. It would benefit some of the local gentry, too. They wouldn't have to ride all the way into Rocheford to borrow a book."

"That would be helpful, I'm sure." Rocheford St. Peters lay only about ten miles away, but ten miles probably seemed a much longer difference if one did not keep a carriage.

"In any case," Frank concluded, "I should be back in time for luncheon."

Hester watched as her brother set out with an umbrella in one hand and a satchel full of books in the other. He walked with a spring in his step, swinging his umbrella back and forth. Strange as it seemed to her, Frank appeared to *like* his life as a country clergyman. The work suited him far better than she would have imagined.

Hester went back into the vicarage, wishing she could borrow some of Frank's cheerful dedication to his labor. She could've used that spirit when it came to the pile of mending she'd promised to work on. She was capable enough with her needle, but mending rips and tears did not fill her with joy the way Frank's work seemed to do.

Fortunately, Rose was perfectly capable of darning stockings while she rested on the sofa. The two women chatted as they worked, though for the most part, Rose talked and Hester listened.

"Everyone keeps asking when the baby will arrive. It gets rather tiresome." Rose put down her work in order to rest a hand on her rounded belly. "One of my friends warned me that would happen, but I thought she exaggerated."

"Was that your friend who lives near Pendle Hill?" Rose corresponded with nearly a dozen different friends, but so far as Hester knew, only one of them had recently delivered a baby.

"Yes, my friend Arabella. She was only two months farther along than I am, so her letters were helpful." A smile broke across Rose's face. "Much more detailed than the letter her husband sent announcing the baby's arrival. He just jotted down the baby's birthday and name and said that Belle was doing well. Can you imagine leaving out all the other information?" She shook her head, looking amused.

What other information did people need? Hester wondered. So far as she knew, one baby looked much like another. Though they probably all looked special in their parents' eyes.

"Anyway," Rose continued, "The Kirkland's' baby, Helena, arrived only a few days after the date of confinement her physician had estimated. That's much better than when Ivy had little Robbie. He was nearly three weeks later than expected! I hope it doesn't run in the family." She pulled a face. "As far as I'm concerned, this little Bracknell is welcome to make an appearance any time now."

"Maybe not today," Hester suggested. "Since the rain might keep the doctor away." They both giggled, then went back to their mending.

Not long after that, a knock at the door put a pause to their work. A visitor? Rose no longer received visitors, except for her relatives. When a housemaid opened the door and ushered Mr. Butler into the room, Rose and Hester exchanged puzzled glances.

Mr. Butler swept a gallant bow. "Ladies, I hope you will forgive the intrusion. I know that Lady Francis is not receiving guests, but I have something to give Lady Hester."

"Something for me?" Hester's eyes widened.

She and Mr. Butler were not on such terms as to justify his giving her any kind of gift. A bouquet of flowers after a ball was the most a gentleman was supposed to give a lady before betrothal. Simon had broken that rule when he gave Hester the garnet pendant, but then, he'd violated propriety right and left during his courtship. The very public good-bye kiss he'd bestowed on her was merely the last of his indiscretions.

"Business took me to Lancaster yesterday," Mr. Butler explained, "and there I found this." He handed her a brown paper package. Then he sat next to her, beaming as he watched her struggle with the tightly-knotted string.

The moment her fingers brushed against the paper wrapping, Hester knew the package contained a book. A small one, though, so probably not a novel. Maybe. . . could it be? Finally, the string snapped. She let it fall to the floor as she unwrapped the paper. Yes, she'd guessed correctly.

"It is Miss Grammar's new collection of poems," she told Rose. "*Lavender and Lilacs.*"

She opened the book, surreptitiously savoring the familiar smell of paper, ink, and binding glue. Her heart skipped a beat when she saw a piece of notepaper pressed between the pages. Had Mr. Butler left some kind of note for her? Good Heavens, what if it was a *billet-doux*? The very idea put a blush on her cheeks.

But she pushed all speculation about the note aside in favor of a more pressing question for Mr. Butler. "Did you really find this in Lancaster?" She'd been certain the book would have to be ordered specially.

But he smiled and nodded. "Quite the merest happenstance! I saw it and immediately thought of you."

She wasn't sure she believed him, although she wanted to. Anyone might see a book and think of someone who liked the author. But if Mr. Butler had gone to the bookstore looking for this book, or worse, had specially ordered it, she could only conclude that he meant to court her in earnest.

Did she want him to court her? Mr. Butler most certainly was handsome, polite, and cultured. A comparison between him and Mr. Haworth popped into her mind unbidden. On the one hand, a good-looking curate who enjoyed poetry. On the other, a tall, slightly gawky solicitor who only read books about medicine and natural history. There really was no comparison. Why, then, did Mr. Butler's gift make Hester uneasy rather than pleased? She should have been glad of the attention.

"Thank you," she said, feeling awkward. She did not know her own mind well enough to know whether she ought to imply "Thank you, I look forward to reading these poems and thinking of your kindness" or "Thank you, but I do not want a suitor right now."

Fortunately, Rose stepped in and helped her out. "It was very kind of you to bring the book over, Mr. Butler, but you'll want to get back to Mrs. Jamison's before the rain begins."

Mr. Butler glanced from Rose to Hester and his smile faded, though he remained as polite as ever. "Quite right. And I know you are in no condition for visitors now, Lady Francis. I will take my leave."

He bowed a farewell to the ladies and Hester held her breath until she heard the front door shut behind him.

"There's a note," Hester told Rose. With trembling fingers, she pulled the slip of folded paper out of the book.

Rose leaned forward, her face alight with interest. "What does the note say?"

Hester broke the seal and unfolded the paper. She bit her lip as she read it, fearing it might be some declaration of love. She sighed with relief when she saw that the note contained no flowery declarations of love—only a list of page numbers and poem titles.

"The note says which poems he particularly liked," she explained to Rose. "Nothing the least bit romantic about it."

She wasn't sure what to make of the fact that he'd apparently read the volume before giving it to her. He might have been trying to impress her. Or he might have been genuinely interested in Miss Grammar's poetry. She had no way of knowing.

"Is he becoming annoying, Hester?" Rose's concern shone out of her soft eyes.

Hester stared down at the book still clutched tightly in her hands. "I don't know," she whispered. "Maybe. Maybe not. I don't know my own mind." She drew a deep breath. "And his intentions are not particularly clear, anyway."

"He is a good-looking and personable young man," Rose pointed out, "but I know little about him beyond that. Frank hired him on the recommendation of a friend from Oxford. I don't know much about Mr. Butler's family. I believe his father is the steward of a large estate in Wiltshire."

"Ah, I see. It is a pity he does not have better prospects." Hester put down the book. His family background might make the decision for her. Her parents would probably not consider Mr. Butler to be a suitable match. Not unless the scandal of being caught with Colonel Lowell was so great that they were willing to marry her off to *anyone* in order to restore her good name.

"I really think I would do better to avoid entanglements right now." Her words were intended as much for herself as for Rose. Her family could not afford any further scandals, which meant she could not afford to make a *mesalliance*. "That seems wise." Rose covered a yawn. "I suppose I'd better take my afternoon nap. Just between you and me, though, I'm tired of lying down all day."

"I don't blame you. I am rather tired of sitting here myself." Hester looked out the window at the overcast day. It had not yet begun to rain. "If you don't mind, I believe I'll take a turn about the garden before the rain starts." Better to get her exercise while she could!

"Very wise." Rose yawned again, adjusted her pillow, and laid back. "You might want to take an umbrella."

Hester grabbed the only remaining umbrella and scurried out the door, half-afraid that the storm would hit before she even reached the garden. But fortune favored her. She reached the gravel path that led around the little plot. Then she slowed down, taking time to savor the rain-scented air. What caused those peculiar smells that heralded rain or snow? Were there men of science who could explain it, or did it remain one of nature's many mysteries?

The vicarage grounds being small, it did not take her long to loop back around to the front garden. There, walking briskly through the gate, was Walter Haworth.

"Lady Hester." He greeted her with a nod. "Do you know if my cousin is at home?"

A grin broke across Hester's face. "Rose is always at home these days. She is not supposed to leave the house, you know." She hesitated for a moment, considering the real question at stake. "She is not supposed to receive visitors, either, but she probably wouldn't mind seeing you. It's just that she happens to be napping at the moment."

"Ah, I ought to have thought of that." He shifted a parcel from one arm to the other.

Hester narrowed her eyes and looked intently at that parcel. Was it her imagination, or did it look like a book? An almost hysterical urge to laugh possessed her as she considered the possibility that Mr. Haworth had also "just happened to see" Maria Grammar's new collection of poems and bought a copy for her.

"If you've a message for Rose I can—" she stopped halfway

through the sentence and lifted her face to the sky. She had just felt the first rain drop. "Or maybe you should come in out of the rain?" Selwyn Castle was less than a mile away, but Mr. Haworth carried no umbrella.

"Oh, there's no need—" A raindrop splashing against his spectacles cut him off mid-sentence. He, too, stared up at the sky. "On second thought, perhaps I ought to step inside until the rain passes."

As if the heavens wanted to show their agreement, the rain began falling in earnest and the fresh scent of petrichor rose from the earth. "Maybe we should hurry." Hester bit back the urge to giggle as they both galloped down the short path from the garden gate to the door of the vicarage.

The moment the door shut behind her, the rain turned into a heavy downpour, the kind that rattled windows and startled sleeping babies. Then she really did start laughing. "I am afraid you picked the wrong afternoon for your visit, Mr. Haworth."

"It couldn't have picked a worse time if I tried," he agreed. "Rose is asleep, and I may be stuck here for an hour. What on earth am I to do while I wait?"

He caught her eye and grinned back at her. His whole face looked sunnier than she'd ever seen it before. Perhaps he was not, after all, the dry, boring lawyer she'd thought him. As for what he was to do—well, she could think of only one answer.

"I think," she suggested, "we had better have a spot of tea."

Chapter Eight

W ALTER HAD TROUBLE wrapping his mind around the fact that Lady Hester had laughed with him. He hadn't realized she was even capable of laughter, at least not genuine, spontaneous laughter. For a moment, she looked and acted like any other young lady of his acquaintance.

By the time they sat down to tea in the dining room, though, Lady Hester had gotten over her fit of giggles. She poured tea and passed the bread and jam with her usual quiet gracefulness. Her mouth quirked up slightly at the corners, showing just a hint of a smile. That was the only remaining sign of good humor.

Still, she seemed much more approachable than she had at any of their past meetings. Walter sat down and chatted with her about Rose's condition, the newly completed preparations to the nursery, and the unexpected rainstorm.

Lady Hester abruptly changed the subject. "Forgive me if the question is impertinent, but does that parcel contain a book?" She nodded in the direction of the brown paper package he'd carried into the house.

"Oh, thank you for reminding me!" Walter's confidence wobbled, but he drew a deep breath and passed the package along to her. "I brought this book because I thought Rose might enjoy hearing it read aloud. I know she finds her confinement tedious." He couldn't imagine how frustrating being confined to a sofa would be, whatever the cause.

For some reason, Lady Hester looked amused rather than pleased. Her lips twitched, and she covered her mouth with one delicate white hand, as if trying to hide her reaction.

"Is this by any chance a book of poems that you merely happened to see while running errands in Lancaster?" A hint of laughter rippled in her voice.

"What?" Walter's eyes widened. What a strangely specific question! "No, it isn't poetry at all. It's the first volume of a novel." He wondered if he'd made a mistake in choosing fiction rather than poetry. But whatever Lady Hester might prefer reading, Rose preferred novels, and he'd been primarily thinking of his cousin when he bought the book.

He pushed the book across the table to Lady Hester. "Of course you may have read it before, though it hasn't been out for very long. I believe it was published this January."

Lady Hester untied the strings binding the package, then carefully unwrapped the paper, rather than tearing into it as Walter might have done. She picked up the book and opened it to the title page.

"*Frankenstein, or the Modern Prometheus,*" she read. "Frankenstein? What a strange name!"

"I believe the name is German, as the novel's protagonist is Genevan by birth," he explained. "Someone told me that there is a Castle Frankenstein in Hesse, though I've never been there."

Understanding lit up her face. "Ah! Is it a Gothic novel, then?"

Walter drew his brows down as he struggled to answer her. "Maybe? It's like Gothic novels in some ways, but different in others. There's a ghastly invention, and some murders, but there are no crumbling castles or deserted abbeys. No ghostly monks or nuns buried alive. It's more philosophical than horrifying."

Lady Hester wrinkled her nose and snapped the book shut. "And you think Rose will be interested in this?" Skepticism colored her voice.

Walter licked his lips nervously. He should have gotten a

book of poetry after all. "I think this novel can provoke many interesting discussions. Whether or not you like it, it offers much to ponder." Good Lord, did he always sound that sententious? As if people read books only to talk about them! Even he knew better than that. "Hopefully, it will be enjoyable, too."

Before Lady Hester could express any more of her doubt, the dining room door swung open. "Walter! If I'd known you planned to visit, I would have stayed awake to greet you."

He sprang to his feet so he could pull out a chair for Rose. "Nonsense. I'm sure you needed your rest." He marveled that she could move at all, given how large she'd gotten, but he kept that thought to himself. He'd learned the hard way that pregnant women did not necessarily like it when other people commented on their increased size.

Lady Hester poured a cup of tea, added a single spoonful of sugar, and passed the cup to Rose, along with a plate of bread and butter. "Your cousin came by to drop off a book for you, but the rain holds him captive," she explained.

Rose took a sip of tea, savoring the taste. Then she smiled at Walter. "So, did you bring us Maria Grammar's latest collection of poems?"

"No!" Walter looked back and forth between the two women, wondering what was so funny. "Am I missing the joke?"

"It's just that Mr. Butler dropped in before my nap to give Hester a book of poetry. I thought you might have had the same idea." Rose glanced askance at Hester, and her smile grew distinctly mischievous. "We think Mr. Butler might fancy Hester."

Warmth flooded Walter's face. "Oh." Did they think he had the same motive? But they must think that, because Lady Hester blushed as she stared into her teacup. "I actually brought this book more for you, Rose. Since you have to spend so much of your time lying down, I mean."

"Oh, how kind of you! Will you read us a chapter or two before you go? Have you time for that?"

He glanced out the window and saw that the rain fell just as heavily as ever. "I have all the time me in the world, it seems. Unless I decide to walk back to the castle in a rainstorm." He didn't much fancy that, especially since he'd been too foolish to think of bringing an umbrella.

"Perfect," Rose declared.

After tea, they all trooped into the parlor. Walter lit a lantern in order to see better. Then he picked up the book and began reading the first of Walton's letters to his sister. He read for half an hour. By then, the rain had slowed to a light pattering.

"I don't suppose I could borrow an umbrella?" he suggested. Rose really wasn't supposed to entertain guests, after all.

"Oh, but you must stay for dinner!" Rose protested.

Lady Hester did not reinforce the request, Walter noticed. Was that because she didn't want him to stay, or merely because she was also a guest in the vicarage, and thus not in a position to invite anyone to dine there?

Walter waffled, wondering if he ought to turn down Rose's invitation. Before he could make up his mind, Frank returned from his errand. He dripped water all over the floor, but seemed in good spirits—. He, too, insisted that Walter had better dine at the vicarage. That finally tipped Walter into accepting the invitation. Frank wouldn't invite him to stay longer if his presence there was in any way bad for Rose.

Dining with Frank and Rose was as pleasant as ever. It might have been Walter's imagination, but he thought Lady Hester seemed more relaxed, less distant, and less cold than in their previous encounters. Perhaps she really wasn't as much of a snob as he'd initially thought.

But after dinner, he ruined whatever rapprochement they had achieved. The trouble began when he saw Lady Hester turning the pages of a little cloth-bound book, with the name Grammar in guilt letters on the spine.

"Is that the new book of poetry you spoke of?" If so, would it be too daring to ask Lady Hester to read a poem or two aloud to him? It would show that Walter was interested in the things that interested her. Though, of course, he could have no reason for wanting to prove that.

"Yes. Mr. Butler remembered me saying that I'd not yet read Miss Grammar's new book, so when he saw a copy of it, he bought it for me." She bit her lip, looking less confident than usual. "At least, so he says."

"But you aren't sure you believe him?" Walter lowered his voice, not wanting Rose or Frank to overhear.

Lady Hester sighed softly. "I hate to accuse a clergyman of lying, but Miss Grammar is a fairly obscure writer. I would be incredibly surprised if a bookseller in Lancaster kept her books stocked. It makes me wonder if Mr. Butler had the seller order the book specially for him." She smiled ruefully. "And if he really did go to all that trouble to get it. . . well, it makes the present mean something a little different, if you know what I mean."

Her pale cheeks blushed a soft shade of pink. For some reason, the phrase "whey-faced chit" popped unbidden into Walter's mind, making him frown. Lady Hester looked as delicately colored as a porcelain figurine. He could not imagine what would have possessed young Mr. What's-His-Name to speak slightingly of her appearance.

Close on the heels of that thought came the memory of Butler's comments about the church livings controlled by the Bracknell family. Why Butler thought those livings would be given to the man who married Lady Hester rather than to Lord Francis, who was also in orders, remained a mystery to Walter. But Butler's obvious mercenary motives constituted a much bigger problem.

Walter looked askance at Lady Hester, wondering how to broach the topic. Fortunately, she gave him the chance he needed.

"I am sure you do not wish to sit here listening to gossip about my potential suitors, Mr. Haworth. That can be of no interest to you."

Walter swallowed nervously, momentarily tongue-tied. "The fact of the matter is. . ." He had no idea how to finish the sentence.

A puzzled line formed between her brows. "Yes? The fact of the matter is what, Mr. Haworth?"

He looked across the room to make certain that neither Rose nor her husband were paying any attention to him. Then he leaned closer to Lady Hester and spoke in a hushed voice. "The fact of the matter is that I overheard Mr. Butler discussing his intentions towards you."

Her eyes widened and her mouth fell ajar. "His intentions?" She closed her mouth, pressing her lips into a tight line. "And what did he say?"

Walter leaned even closer so he could murmur directly in her ear. "He certainly sounded interested in courting you, but his primary motive seemed to be financial. He mentioned that the Bracknell family controls three clerical livings, and said your attraction was 'the appeal of a steady income.'"

"Excuse me?" She drew her head back sharply.

Realizing that he was much too close for good manners, Walter moved back, too. "I am sorry if I offend. I just thought you ought to know how mercenary his motives are. But perhaps you don't intend to encourage his courtship anyway, which—" It was almost a relief when she interrupted his panicked babbling.

"I believe I can do better than to marry a poor curate," she snapped. "And I assure you, it takes more than a book of poetry to win my affections." She curled her lip disdainfully.

But when Walter lowered his eyes, he saw that her clasped hands were shaking, though he could not tell whether rage or fear triggered their trembling. It was clear, though, that his words had shaken her.

"I apologize for giving advice that you may neither have needed or wanted." He'd fallen back into his most formal, priggish tones, and he inwardly cringed at how stuffy he sounded. "I only wanted to help."

"I thank you, but your assistance is not needed." Lady Hester bit off each word, creating a staccato effect that made Walter cringe.

"Again, I am very sorry." He wished he'd kept his mouth shut. Better yet, he wished he'd never even overheard Butler talking about his matrimonial schemes. "I ought to have minded my own business."

"Indeed." She pointedly looked away from him. Her rigid posture radiated indignation.

Walter glanced out the window at the darkening sky, then rose from his chair and stretched. The motion caught the attention of Rose and Frank, who looked in his direction for the first time in half an hour.

"I believe the rain has stopped," Walter announced. "I ought to take my leave now, before I lose the last of the light." This wasn't merely an excuse; he really didn't fancy a walk alone in the dark.

"I suppose you ought," Rose agreed. "But thank you for dropping in, Walter. It is pleasant to have company when I am stuck at home."

"Thank you very much for inviting me to dine on such short notice." He glanced down at Lady Hester. "And thank you for your company, ma'am." He offered her a slight bow, hoping that might appease her anger.

"You are very welcome, Mr. Haworth." Neither Lady Hester's brittle smile nor her cool voice supported her words.

But Walter supposed that was the best he could hope for. He'd stuck his nose where it didn't belong, and he had no one to blame but himself. Next time he heard some unsavory bit of gossip related to Lady Hester, he would keep it to himself.

Chapter Nine

THE WORST THING about Mr. Haworth's warning was that Hester suspected he'd told her nothing but the truth. In the coming days, Mr. Butler continued to show signs that he might be trying to fix his interest with Hester. He dropped in at the vicarage daily, ostensibly to check up on Rose's health. But he always spent more time talking to Hester than he did Rose.

The thirteenth of June was Hester's birthday, and Lord and Lady Inglewhite planned a party to celebrate. Hester initially assumed that this would merely mean dining at the castle, but she soon learned that they had hired a few local musicians so the young people could have a dance after dinner.

When Hester protested that she didn't need so grand a celebration just because she was turning twenty, Lady Inglewhite dismissed her objections. "Since we have a ballroom, we might as well put it to use! What's the point in having a room dedicated to dancing if no one ever dances?"

Hester could hardly argue with that. She did not particularly want to argue, anyway. After weeks of country life, she looked forward to a chance to don a ball gown and show off her pearls.

On the thirteenth of June, Hester came back from her afternoon walk to find a bouquet of pink and white roses waiting for her. She picked up the bouquet and sniffed, enjoying the rich floral scent.

But when she opened up the folded scrap of notepaper, she saw that the flowers were from Mr. Butler. That didn't exactly surprise her, but it did disappoint her. She would rather not even think about her unwanted suitor on today of all days. She'd hoped the flowers had been ordered by someone in her family—her mother, maybe. It would have been nice to have some indication that her parents thought about her on the anniversary of her birth. Instead, she hadn't even received a letter from them.

She sighed, then brought the flowers into the parlor to show Rose.

"Oh dear," Rose said. "It's a lovely bouquet, but you don't look at all happy about it."

Hester nodded grimly. "Unfortunately, I do not return Mr. Butler's affections," she admitted. "If he declares himself, I will reject him."

She didn't know when she'd come to that decision, but she felt confident about it. Hester's frequent megrims sometimes made socializing difficult, which in turn made it hard to attract a suitor. That was part of why her first season in London had been unsuccessful: she'd often had to cancel invitations to drive in Hyde Park or attend the theater with a gentleman. Even so, that didn't mean Hester needed to marry the first honorable man who proposed to her.

Mr. Butler's mercenary motives weren't even her primary objection to him. Even if Mr. Haworth were wrong about Mr. Butler having his eye on the Bracknell family livings, Hester would not have accepted him. Over the last two weeks, Hester had seen enough of Mr. Butler to realize that though he was an attractive and gallant suitor, she did not want to spend the rest of her life with him. She wasn't even sure she wanted to spend an hour alone with him. His compliments and courtesies had begun to ring hollow, as had the platitudes he enjoyed repeating.

Selfishly, Hester hoped Mr. Butler would not attend tonight's birthday celebration at Selwyn Castle. If he asked her to dance, she would have no reason to refuse. Under other circumstances, she would not at all have minded standing up with him for the duration of a country dance. Now, she feared that dancing with the curate would only encourage his courtship.

Still, she looked forward to the party. It gave her an excuse to don her newest ball gown, which consisted of a pink satin underdress and an overdress of white gauze, embroidered at the sleeves, hem, and neckline with a darker pink. It had been made in the latest mode, so it had the highest waist and tiniest bodice of any dress she'd ever worn. Rose arranged Hester's hair, piling it on top of her head and encircling it with a bandeau that matched the embroidery on her gown.

"They say turbans are all the rage this year," Rose commented. "Is that true?"

Hester made a face. "Yes, but I don't like turbans. I refuse to wear one. I think this looks well enough." She studied herself in the mirror, wondering if she'd made a mistake. "Doesn't it?" she asked anxiously.

"Of course, it looks well enough," Rose assured her. "You look lovely tonight." She startled Hester by pressing a light kiss against her cheek. "Now, go break the hearts of all the young gentlemen in a ten-mile radius."

Hester had to laugh at that suggestion. "I wish you could come with us."

But Rose shook her head firmly. "Even if my doctor were in favor of it, I wouldn't want to go. I would feel tired and miserable and want to go home. It would end with me dragging you and Frank away from the party early. And we can't have that, can we? You two will enjoy yourselves more without me there."

Hester wasn't sure about that, but she still climbed into the carriage with a light heart. Normally, the Bracknell family walked back and forth between the vicarage and the castle, but both the late hour and the delicacy of Hester's dancing slippers made that inadvisable. Once again, the earl and the countess had sent a carriage down to the vicarage. Hester rode in luxury to the castle, and felt like a princess when the groom helped her step down from the carriage.

There was, of course, no red carpet spread from the front door to the carriage sweep, as there might have been at a London townhouse. Even so, Hester felt proud to walk into the Great Hall of the castle on Frank's arm. Was there another gentleman half so distinguished as her brother? Maybe the Earl of Inglewhite, but he was so much older than Frank that he hardly counted.

For the first half hour, Hester thoroughly enjoyed herself. She'd already met most of the guests. Others were introduced to her, including a handful of young ladies close to her in age.

These young ladies studied Hester from head to toe. She suspected they were taking in all the details of her London fashions. None of them seemed to be dressed in the latest modes favored by the *haute ton*. Nor did Hester have any idea about what to say to them. She did not know enough about local society to know what questions to ask, nor did she have any interesting gossip of her own to share.

Then one of the Miss Andersons (Hester could not remember her given name) broke the awkward silence by asking if it was true that turbans were in style in London.

Hester grimaced. "Yes, but I've always thought they look ridiculous. My mother wanted me to wear one, but I refused."

"I think they are better suited to older women, anyway," confided the other Miss Anderson. "I *would* like to wear a tiara someday, though."

"The only time I have worn a tiara was when I was presented at Court," Hester admitted. "My mother thinks they are too flashy for an unmarried woman."

"That sounds like the sort of thing my mother would say, too," Miss Anderson replied.

The mournfulness in her voice reminded Hester of the way Julia complained about maternal edicts. The corner of her mouth twitched as she suppressed a smile. After that, conversation was easy, and the young ladies chattered happily together until the orchestra struck up the tune for a country dance.

Because the party was being held to celebrate Hester's birthday, Lord Inglewhite himself stood up with her in the first set. Though he was no taller than Hester, the earl wore an air of gravity that gave him an intimidating presence—at least, until he smiled at her. Then his whole face softened, making him look much more approachable.

The rest of the party went smoothly. Lord and Lady Inglewhite did not keep Town hours, of course, so the party broke up for supper at nine. That was when the trouble began. Mr. Butler had arrived late, so Hester had managed to avoid him for the first half of the evening, but he claimed the first set after supper.

After their set ended, he peered down at Hester and shook his head. "You look flushed, my dear. Do you need to step out of the room for a breath of fresh air?"

Hester frowned. "I thank you, no." She darted her eyes around the room, looking for some means of escape. "If you would be so kind as to fetch me a glass of lemonade, that ought to cool me."

To her relief, he hurried away to get the drink. By the time he returned, she was already dancing with young Mr. Anderson, who was home from Cambridge on the Long Vacation. She felt relieved to have escaped the curate's unwanted attentions.

But Mr. Butler merely bided his time. As soon as her set with Mr. Anderson concluded, Mr. Butler approached with her lemonade. Hester forced a cool smile to her face, trying to act as if she'd forgotten all about her desire for a drink.

All of her composure shattered in an instant when the drink tipped over in his hand, splashing the front of her dress. She gasped and stared down in shock. How had that happened?

Mr. Butler gasped. "I am so very clumsy! Please, let me escort you to the lady's retiring room." He sounded so appropriately dismayed that Hester abandoned her fleeting suspicion that he might have spilled the drink on purpose.

Because she couldn't remember where the lady's retiring room was, Hester had no choice but to follow Mr. Butler out of the ballroom. There could be no impropriety involved, she told herself, since it wasn't as if Mr. Butler would actually enter the room with her. And anyway, there'd be an attendant in the retiring room.

They walked down the corridor until he opened a door and gestured for her to walk in.

She stepped into the room and looked around for the supplies typically provided for the use of ladies who needed to mend a torn hem or adjust a damaged coiffure. None of the usual accouterments of a retiring room were visible. She saw only a few pieces of furniture covered with drop-clothes, some half-empty bookshelves along the walls, and a slate board that gave away the purpose of the room.

"This isn't the retiring room," she said. "This is a school room." What a strange mistake for Mr. Butler to make!

"Yes, but here we can be sure of no interruptions," Mr. Butler explained. "That makes it ideal."

He shut the door, then leaned against it, effectively blocking the way out. They were alone in a room: a compromising situation if ever she saw one. Hester took a cautious step backward and cast her eyes around the room, looking for an escape route. But there was nowhere for her to go. Mr. Butler still barred the only exit. He crossed his arms and casually leaned one foot back, looking for all the world as if he were settling in for a lengthy conversation.

"What are you doing?" The waver in Hester's voice dismayed her. She could do better than that! Before her captor could answer her, she tried again. "I must insist that you stand aside so I can leave the room." That sounded more confident!

"By and by," he promised. "I will not detain you for long, but I wish to speak to you."

"You can have nothing to say to me, sir. I am not interested in any proposals you might wish to make." Hester did not even try to keep the anger out of her voice. She had every right to be angry, after the way he had tricked her into being alone with him.

"Oh, I think I have something to say, my lady." One side of his mouth curved up in a predatory half-smile. "You may not be interested in my proposals now, but it's only a matter of time before someone comes looking for you. When they find you alone in here with me, you'll look at my offer in quite a different light."

Hester's eyes widened, and her hands began to tremble. "You are trying to force my hand by deliberately compromising me? That is *despicable*."

Mr. Butler arched his eyebrows. "Compromising you will not be necessary if you'll listen to reason, my lady. You have a good deal to gain from an alliance with me."

Oh, really? Unable to think of words sufficiently venomous for this situation, Hester sneered at her captor. He smirked in return, and drew a deep breath, as if preparing to lecture her. Before he could speak, though, someone rattled the doorknob from outside the room.

"I say. Is everything all right in there?" Muffled by the door, the voice was unidentifiable, but Hester knew one thing: she and her would-be bridegroom were no longer alone.

Chapter Ten

A MIXTURE OF desperation and embarrassment swirled in Walter's stomach as he pounded on the door. He'd seen Neville Butler and Lady Hester disappear into the old schoolroom together. He knew perfectly well that Butler's courtship was none of his business, but his doubts about Butler's integrity made him linger in the corridor. . . just in case. In case of what? He had no clear idea.

He lurked a few feet away from the room, feeling very foolish, until the sound of a voice raised in anger or fear called him into action. He'd expected the door to swing open at the turn of the knob, but something or someone held it shut. That only increased his concern.

"I say, is everything all right in there?" He shouted, not knowing how well his voice would carry through the solid wooden door.

Lady Hester responded by shouting *"Help!"*

That did it! Walter lunged at the door, slamming it with his shoulder. Maybe he hit it a little too hard, because the door flew open and Walter stumbled into the room, crashing into Butler.

"What the hell are you doing here, Haworth?" Butler snapped. "This is a private conversation."

For once, Walter's glasses genuinely needed to be straightened. That gave him a moment to catch his breath. "When a gentleman hears a young lady calling for help, he answers the call." He glared at Butler, then turned toward Lady Hester.

He could see no signs of physical injury, but Lady Hester leaned against the desk at the front of the room, looking as if her knees were too weak to hold her up. A few cautious steps brought Walter to her side. She seemed to be trembling with fear or shock. Had he known her better, he might've reassured her with a comforting touch, but that didn't seem proper.

Instead, he leaned over her. "Lady Hester, are you well? Do you require medical attention?"

"Medical attention!?" Butler said scornfully. "I haven't so much as touched her. We were merely talking about a *private* matter." He very nearly growled the last few words.

"You don't have to touch a person to hurt them!" Walter snapped. Then he winced at the bite in his own voice. He'd better get his temper under control. He drew a deep breath and slowly released it, counting to three.

Walter cleared his throat and tried a less impassioned approach. "I think you had better leave the room, Mr. Butler. You have caused Lady Hester enough distress for one night."

Butler raised his eyebrows. "And leave *you* alone here with her? That would be most improper and most unfair, since I was here first."

Walter clenched his hands into fists. "We will leave the door open, so there will be no impropriety. But if you are worried about the situation, you may fetch—" he paused to think of who could best comfort Lady Hester.

Had Rose been here, he might have relied on her, since Lady Hester seemed to get along well with her. But though Lady Hester's sister-in-law was not at the castle tonight, she did have a cousin at hand.

"You may tell Lady Inglewhite that she is needed in here," Walter said.

"And Frank," Lady Hester whispered. "I would like to talk to Frank."

"Very well." Butler stalked out of the room in a fit of pique.

The door slammed shut behind the curate, but true to his word, Walter opened it up again, using the nearest chair to keep it from swinging shut. With the door propped open, a faint murmur of voices drifted in from the ballroom, reminding them that the other guests were only a stone's throw away.

Walter ran a hand through his hair and sighed. "I am very sorry that you have been so ill-treated, my lady." The words didn't seem at all adequate, but he doubted there was anything he could say that *would* be adequate. "Are you sure he did you no harm?"

Lady Hester gulped, but remained silent. Judging from the way her hands trembled, she seemed to be in a state of shock. Walter silently brought her a chair. She cast a grateful look at him as she sank down on it. She rested a moment before answering him.

"He didn't hurt me, but he frightened me." She spoke so softly, he had to lean in to catch her words. "He was trying to compromise me so that I'd have to marry him."

Walter's jaw dropped. He shut it quickly, not wanting to gape, but he could hardly believe what he'd heard. "I had no idea he was such a scoundrel."

Or had he known? He'd suspected Neville Butler of embezzling money from a charitable institution. He'd known that Butler courted Lady Hester primarily for mercenary motives. Was it really so surprising that he was guilty of other dishonorable actions?

"I had no idea, either," Lady Hester said. "You were right to warn me about him."

Walter could only shake his head. "I thought he was only a fortune hunter. I wouldn't have thought him capable of such manipulation." The more he thought about it, the angrier he got. Her whole life could have been ruined! "Perhaps you ought to pursue legal action against him."

She lifted her eyes up, surprised. "On what grounds? It's not as if he assaulted me or kidnapped me. I suppose he did threaten me, but he wasn't threatening bodily harm. . ."

"I think marrying someone against their will implies bodily harm," Walter argued.

He set his mouth in a grim line as he contemplated Butler's threat. A woman forced into accepting an unwanted suitor was unlikely to have a happy marriage—and that was putting it mildly. A man who would force her hand when it came to a proposal probably wouldn't respect her desires on other issues, either.

Before he could say more, though, they were interrupted by the arrival of both Frank and Ivy.

"Hetty? Are you ill?" her brother demanded. "Mr. Butler said you wanted us immediately?"

"Has something happened?" Ivy sounded anxious, as well she ought to be. She lifted her eyes up to meet Walter's gaze. "Do you know what this is about?"

He made a quick decision. "I do, but I think an explanation might best come from Hester herself. I believe I ought to step out of the room and give you some privacy."

"Yes, please." Lady Hester had stopped trembling. She held her brother's hand, her knuckles white with pressure. "I would appreciate that."

Walter nodded and left her to explain the situation. Only after he walked away did he realize that he'd addressed Lady Hester by her given name alone, without her title. How presumptuous of him! She would think him no better than Butler.

And what was he going to do about Butler? Lady Hester was probably right that the bounder had not given her clear grounds for any kind of criminal action. It might be illegal for a man to coerce a woman into marrying him, but it would be difficult to prove that he'd threatened her. It would be her word against his. Since the man in this case was a respected clergyman, it might be hard to convince a judge that he was guilty of something so underhanded.

All the more reason why Walter needed to solve the embezzlement case, and soon. If Butler were really guilty, he must be stopped before he repeated his crime. And the more Walter learned about the man, the more possible it seemed that Butler might be the criminal Walter was looking for.

It was time, Walter decided, to go back to the Haworth Home and see for himself what Ernest Robinson had discovered. Ernest might very well have confidential information that he did not want to put in writing. And even if Ernest hadn't learned anything, Walter could use him as a sounding board.

FORTUNATELY, THE WEATHER cooperated with Walter's travel plans. Though gray clouds covered the sky, the pending rain held off until after Walter reached the parsonage at the home. Ernest and Frederic were surprised to see him, but pleased.

After dinner, Walter followed Ernest into his study for a private conversation. Walter pulled an old leather armchair closer to his brother-in-law's desk. He sat down, leaned his head back, and closed his eyes. A gentleman's study was supposed to smell of old books and tobacco, but this evening, the lattice window let in a light breeze from the outdoors. Walter drew in a deep breath of spring air.

Ernest seated himself behind his desk, but he leaned back in the chair and propped his feet up on top of the desk. Then he ran a hand through his short curls. Ernest came from quite a different background than the family he'd married into. His father had been English, but his mother had been a free woman of color from the French Antilles. Like many West Indian traders and plantation owners, Elias Robinson had sent his natural children to England to be educated. Ernest spoke and acted like any other member of the gentry class, but people in rural Somerset were sometimes prejudiced against him.

This prejudice had never stopped Ernest from doing his duty. Today, for instance, he did indeed have news for Walter. "I meant to write to you about my progress with the ledgers," he explained, "but we had a nasty case of measles go through the home, and things were rather hectic."

Walter stiffened in his chair. Measles was a killer, and it spread like lightning. "Did the orphanage lose any of the children?"

Ernest nodded. "An infant foundling and a three-year old. One of the older children seems to have lost his sight, but he will otherwise recover." The bleakness of his tone hinted at how devastating these losses had been. "Unfortunately, the outbreak isn't yet over. You had better not go up to the main building this visit."

"Good Lord! I had no idea. I would not have burdened you with an unexpected guest if I'd any idea you were dealing with this." Walter felt like kicking himself. Why hadn't he simply written to Ernest with his questions?

Ernest sighed. "No one *here* is sick yet. Luckily, Freddy and I both had measles as children. We've been keeping Ned away from all the children, even the ones who seem healthy." He grimaced. "Miss Miller thought we might as well let him catch the disease and get it over with, but he's only just three years old, and we'd rather not risk it."

"Of course not!" Walter was horrified at the thought of deliberately allowing a small child to catch a deadly disease. Did people do that? "Anyway, I can see you've got your hands full, so I'll be out of here as soon as I can. I only wanted to know if you'd made any kind of progress studying the handwriting."

To his surprise, Ernest nodded. "As a matter of fact, we did. I had Mr. Hunt up here. He teaches penmanship, you know, and someone told me he knew a fair bit about handwriting. He took a look at the ledgers, and—well, I might just as well show you."

Ernest got up from his chair, walked over to the wall, and removed a handsome seascape in a gilt frame, revealing a wall safe. He unlocked it and took out a couple of ledgers. He brought the books over to Walter and opened one up in the middle.

"Take a look at the lines underlined in pencil," he suggested.

Walter adjusted his glasses and obediently took a look. It took a moment for him to even find the underlining. On the left page, only one line had been underlined. On the right page, there were three.

"What am I supposed to be seeing?" Walter asked. It was hard to read the writing at all, but one line appeared to list a payment for two dozen woolen socks. Another listed an order of potatoes. "Ah, I remember this one. It's one of the earliest fraudulent charges, isn't it?" He pointed to the potato's entry.

That had been one of the first discrepancies Miss Miller noticed, and she'd only noticed it because she happened to be looking over expenses the day before Farmer Bright delivered two crates of potatoes. A chance conversation with the farmer revealed that he'd been charging the same price per pound for the last five years, which meant the entry in the ledger was wrong.

At first Miss Miller assumed the discrepancy between the actual price and the recorded price was due to some minor error. After she'd found several such "errors," she'd gone to the board with the news that someone had falsified expense accounts for months.

"Yes. To be clear, not all the underlined expenses are fraudulent. But they're all written in the same handwriting. And Mr. Hunt is certain it *isn't* Mrs. Fairfax's writing."

A frisson of anticipation swept from Walter's head to his feet. They were on the right track. He *knew* it. "Are all the fraudulent entries written in this hand, then?"

"That's hard to tell. There are a few that are ambiguous. Hunt thinks the crook might have been testing out different styles of writing. Trying to make it hard to identify them by writing."

Of course it had to be difficult, Walter thought bitterly. Nothing could ever be easy.

"So, can we eliminate Mrs. Fairfax from our list of suspects?"

That would be some progress.

"Probably." Ernest sighed again. "It's theoretically possible that she knew about the theft, but winked at it or ignored it. But it looks like she wasn't the one directly involved in falsifying the ledger entries."

"I doubt she knew anything," Walter guessed. "So, who does that leave us with? Is Neville Butler still a suspect?"

"We can't rule him out." Ernest frowned. "Hunt says he doesn't have a good enough sample of his writing to tell either way."

"You'd think there'd be any number of notes or letters from Butler still in the office," Walter suggested.

"You most certainly would think that, wouldn't you? But there's almost nothing in his hand. Rather makes me wonder, to be honest."

Ernest and Walter exchanged a look laden with meaning. Butler seemed to be an intelligent man. If he were the one embezzling money, he might have done his best to avoid leaving samples of his handwriting behind when he left the home.

Walter thought back to his interview with the curate. "Butler claims both Mrs. Johnson and Miss Eversley sometimes handled the accounts. Is that true?"

Ernest made a face. "Only very rarely. Mrs. Johnson's writing is unmistakable. She always printed her entries in large, blocky letters. She doesn't know how to write in cursive, so she can be ruled out. Miss Eversley is trickier. She has quite excellent writing—clear and readable. It doesn't look much like the falsified entries, but of course, she could have been deliberately disguising her writing."

"As could anyone." Walter rested his head in his hands, momentarily overwhelmed by the difficulty of the task before them. "But I agree that it's suspicious that Butler didn't leave many samples of his handwriting behind. I'll have to see if Frank—Lord Francis, I mean—has anything in his hand. Seems as if he ought to have something!"

Ernest's face brightened. "That would be a great help." He

narrowed his eyes. "Something else bothering you, Walter?"

"Yessss." Walter dragged out the word. He'd rather not admit this, but it might need to be said. "The problem is, I don't think that I'm capable of being objective when it comes to Neville Butler. Not anymore." He scowled as he recalled the look of panic he saw in Lady Hester's eyes when he broke into the schoolroom and found her alone with Butler.

Ernest raised his eyebrows. "It sounds like there's a story there," he said cautiously. "Is it one you can tell?"

"I suppose I'd better." Walter stared down at the open ledger as he explained his most recent encounters with Neville Butler, including the overheard discussion about dowries and church livings, as well as Butler's attempt to compromise Lady Hester to force her to marry him. By the time he finished speaking, Ernest's eyes had widened considerably.

"Good Heavens," he said faintly. "He really is a knave, isn't he?"

Walter nodded, but held his tongue. If he started saying what he really thought about Neville Butler, it might end in an incoherent stream of invective. That was how angry the man made him.

"That makes it seem all the more likely that he could be our thief, since he's clearly capable of unethical behavior." Ernest sounded almost hopeful.

"Yes, but that might also mean that we're biased against him," Walter pointed out. "Or at least I am. I'd like to have him thrown in Newgate for something. But I don't want to let my anger cloud my judgment." He had too much reason to want Butler to be found guilty.

"I do see the problem." A wrinkle formed on Ernest's brow, and he rested his head on his hand as he thought. "But of all the men I know, you are the least likely to indulge in a fit of bad temper."

Walter smiled grimly. "Let's hope it stays that way." Though he normally prided himself on his rational thinking, he could not trust his temper when it came to Neville Butler.

Chapter Eleven

AFTER HER ILL-FATED birthday party, Hester felt like a child who'd inadvertently kicked a hornet's nest. By the time they got back to the vicarage, Frank was spitting with anger. He must have woken Rose up in order to tell her about it, because Rose tapped at Hester's door to see if she needed anything.

"A cup of hot milk?" Rose suggested. "A shoulder to cry on?" She stood in the doorway, rubbing sleep crusts out of her eyes.

"I'm fine. You can go back to sleep." Hester hoped her smile didn't look as fragile as it felt.

"If you need anything, you have only to ask," Rose promised.

Hester lay in bed for what seemed like hours, unable to sleep. Her mind wouldn't stop racing. Over and over again, she remembered the look of cool confidence on Mr. Butler's face when he explained his plan to compromise her.

How could he have expected his plot to work? Even if he'd succeeded in forcing her to accept his proposal, her family would have been furious. There was no way Hester's father would give any of the family livings to someone who manipulated his daughter into an unwanted marriage! Nor would he have agreed to marriage settlements that favored Mr. Butler.

Besides, the curate had forgotten something important: there was more than one way to restore a woman's reputation through marriage. Another scandal on top of the Colonel Lowell incident would have been devastating, yes, but the damage could have been mitigated if she quickly married a gentleman of good repute. She need not marry Butler; any respectable gentleman would do. Nothing restored a broken reputation as well as matrimony did!

But marrying a stranger merely for the sake of preserving her good name didn't seem much more appealing than marriage to a scoundrel. She supposed she would do it if it were the only way to keep from dishonoring the family name, but she hoped it wouldn't come to that. Now more than ever, she wanted something better out of marriage. During her visit to Ingleton, Hester had seen for herself how a marriage of affection could work. Far from convincing her to avoid love matches, it had made such a marriage seem ideal.

Frank and Rose did not always see eye-to-eye, but they clearly cared about each other. They worked well together, too, in part because they were both good-tempered, not prone to quarrelling. Frank's desire to help people encouraged Rose to use her talents to benefit the parish, while Rose's playful spirits seemed to cheer Frank up after a hard or boring day.

In the span of a few weeks, Hester had gone from pitying her brother and his wife for their cramped quarters and modest style of living to envying them for their comfortable relationship. It had never before occurred to her that "comfort" was not necessarily synonymous with "luxury."

If she was honest with herself, she knew it was unlikely that she and Simon Lowell would have enjoyed anything like this cozy domesticity even if they'd been able to marry. Could husbands who liked quiet and comfort even be found among the drawing rooms and ballrooms of the *ton*? She had her doubts. Such men probably didn't come to London, or avoided the activities of the season. How one could arrange to meet such a man, she did not know. She only knew that Rose and Frank were fortunate to have met at Lord Inglewhite's house party two years ago.

The next day, Hester saw just how much trouble her encounter with Mr. Butler had caused. Frank called the curate into his study in order to sack him. Mr. Butler left the study looking thoroughly abashed. He discomfited Hester by stopping in front of her and bowing.

"Lady Hester, I am deeply sorry for having made you so uncomfortable last night. My jest got out of hand. I assure you that it was an ill-planned joke rather than a genuine threat. I would never have actually tried to trap an unwilling young lady into matrimony!" His dark eyes, brimming with apparent contrition, importuned her forgiveness.

Hester held her breath, wavering between two impulses. She did not for one moment believe Mr. Butler, and she could not decide whether to tell him so. Though she would rather have read him a lecture on the proper treatment of women, she reluctantly decided that good manners required her to accept his apology, however insincere she believed it to be.

"Thank you for explaining yourself, Mr. Butler. I am relieved to learn that I misunderstood your intentions. Though I cannot return your affections, I hope we may remain on good terms." She could not bring herself to utter the words "I forgive you," or to wish that they might remain friends. She did not want to be his friend!

"Of course, my lady. Rest assured I would never make the mistake of so insulting you again!" Butler bowed again before walking briskly out the door. She wished she could believe him!

Unfortunately, Hester learned, Mr. Butler did not intend to leave town immediately. Frank would be out of town for a week, so he needed Butler to cover all the church services next Sunday.

"I wish I could've sent him packing today," Frank explained, "but I do need him this week. Besides, he's already paid for a month's lodgings. He may need to stay at Mrs. Jamison's house while he works out his next plans." He twisted his face into a grimace. "I know little about Neville's family, except that they are not wealthy. He will have to seek a new position as curate, and it may be hard to do so without a letter of reference—which, of course, I would never give him after the way he treated you."

Hester shook her head, surprised by her brother. Frank sounded almost sympathetic towards Mr. Butler. But when she considered how her life could have been altered if Mr. Butler's plan had succeeded, she could not bring herself to care whether or not he found a new position. For all she cared, he could go pick oakum in the nearest workhouse, so long as he left soon. She did not feel comfortable walking abroad alone while he remained at Ingleton.

A FEW NIGHTS later, the sound of someone pounding on the vicarage door yanked Hester out of slumber. She sat up and shook her head, momentarily confused. She'd been dreaming of a visit to Vauxhall, of all places. In her dream, she stood by Simon's side as fireworks burst overhead. The loud knock on the front door had merged with the boom of the fireworks, making it hard for Hester to tell the dream from reality.

As she woke up and realized where she was, she remembered her final, fateful encounter with Simon in the Duke of Creighton's garden. There had been fireworks that night, too. Hester's heart ached as she recalled the pain of learning that Simon, whom she fully expected to marry, had married an heiress without even telling Hester beforehand.

As if marrying someone else without warning had not been bad enough, Simon had the audacity to ask Hester for a goodbye kiss. "Such dear friends as we may kiss each other good-bye when fate pulls them apart, mayn't they?" he'd said.

Hester should have known that kissing a married man was wrong. Had she thought about it with a mind unclouded by emotion, she would have realized how demeaning it was for Simon to refer to her as a "friend," when in fact, they had been sweethearts.

Though Simon had never officially proposed to Hester, she'd

allowed him far more liberties than a young lady ought to give her fiancé. They'd shared many stolen kisses and private embraces; in fact, he'd come close to ruining her. After all that passed between them, for Simon to turn around and marry a girl with a larger dowry was beyond insulting. It was almost evil.

But the night of the Creighton ball, none of those things had occurred to Hester. She'd thought only of her love for Simon, and of the grief she would feel now that they must be forever parted. She'd assumed that in a dark corner of the garden, none of the other guests would see what they were doing.

So, she had tipped her face up for Simon's last kiss. At first, he had pressed his mouth against hers lightly, almost chastely. Then he'd wrapped an arm around her and drew her body against his. Their embrace had been oh so sweet, until fireworks had started bursting.

Not figurative fireworks. Real ones. Hester had pulled her mouth away from Simon's and tipped her head back to stare up at the pyrotechnic display. Red and gold flowers arched gracefully through the sky, making brief, brilliant constellations, only to fall in sparkling showers. Behind her, she'd heard the familiar "Oooh!" of spectators delighted by the fiery show. And that's when she realized that she and Simon were not alone. Their adulterous kiss had been observed by at least a dozen members of the *bon ton*. Now, revisiting that scandalous moment nearly two months later, Hester looked back with a mixture of regret and relief. Regret for the mistakes she'd made with Simon: relief that she had not married him after all. Given that Simon had been willing to kiss Hester while married to another woman, what was to say that he would have been faithful to Hester if they'd married each other? Poor Eliza Prescott had been married to him for only a few days before he violated his marriage vows!

Hester shook her head, dismissing those painful reflections. Once she paid attention to her surroundings, she heard raised voices coming from downstairs. She slipped out of bed, donned her dressing gown, and hurried downstairs.

She found Rose in the foyer, staring out the open door. Rose covered her mouth with one hand, looking distraught.

"What is it?" But Hester didn't need to wait for the answer. When she stared down the lane that led into the rest of the village, she saw a bright glow, like a bonfire, but larger. "A house fire?"

"Yes. Mrs. Jamison's house," Rose explained. "That poor woman!" She shook her head.

Something niggled at the back of Hester's mind. She'd heard the name "Jamison" before, though she couldn't remember why. She set that puzzle aside in favor of more immediate concerns. "Should we go join the villagers?"

It must have been past midnight, but the full moon cast a bright light over the village green, where the entire population of Ingleton seemed to be clustered. Hester could not make out any faces, of course, just dark forms silhouetted against the blazing fire.

"Frank told me to stay here," Rose admitted. "I suppose you are welcome to go watch the fire from up close if you prefer—"

"No." Hester hadn't meant for them to be mere spectators. "I just thought there might be something we ought to be doing to help. Hauling buckets of water, perhaps?"

She'd never witnessed a house fire before, but she had the vague idea that lots of water would be needed to combat it, since there were no fire engines in a village this small. In fact, that might be why everyone had gathered in the village green. There was a water pump in the green.

"Oh!" Rose looked down at her round belly and wrinkled her nose. "Maybe. I don't think I'd be of much use waddling back and forth with buckets of water, though."

"No, I suppose not." Hester came very close to giggling as she imagined Rose trying to put the fire out. At this stage of her pregnancy, merely going up stairs made her struggle to catch her breath. The way Rose's eyes crinkled at the corners suggested Hester wasn't alone in her amusement.

"You are welcome to go if you wish, but I believe I ought to stay here," Rose said.

"I doubt I would be of much use, either," Hester admitted. She was neither particularly fast nor particularly strong, and she'd certainly never helped put out a fire before. She might very well get in the way of more competent helpers.

Rose smiled at her. "In any case, I would appreciate your company while I wait for Frank to return. And I may even need you here, if any of Mrs. Jamison's lodgers need shelter for the night."

"Lodgers?" Ah, that was the memory that had been teasing Hester! "Mrs. Jamison is the woman who rents out rooms, isn't she?"

Rose nodded. "It's very unfortunate that the fire struck her house, of all places. I don't know where she'll go or what she'll do! Her husband left her with little but her house, so she supported herself by taking in lodgers. She won't be able to earn money that way now."

"Oh." That hadn't occurred to Hester at all. Naively, she'd assumed that as long as everyone escaped the fire unharmed, all would be well. Houses could be rebuilt, after all. But how was a widow with no income supposed to rebuild her home?

Something else occurred to her, too, as she thought about Mrs. Jamison's lodgers. "Isn't that where Mr. Butler lodges?" So far as she knew, Mrs. Jamison was the only villager who took in lodgers. Most people did not have the extra rooms.

"It was where he lodged, yes." Rose's voice was flat, and Hester could get no sense of how she felt about that.

"I suppose he was going to leave town anyway," Hester mused. "So perhaps it is not a great loss to him." Was it too much to hope that the fire would drive him out of town earlier? Her heart suddenly lifted at that idea.

A moment later, she sternly reminded herself that she ought not be glad about the fire. A woman had lost her home and her livelihood. It was a terrible thing! But Hester hoped that perhaps this meant the last she'd seen of Neville Butler.

She and Rose sat in the parlor, looking out the window to watch the fire for what seemed like hours. Hester leaned back in her chair and began to close her eyes for longer and longer periods. Rose yawned loudly enough to wake the sleeping souls in the churchyard.

"Maybe you should go to bed?" Hester suggested. She understood that Rose wanted to be on hand in case her help was needed, but it probably wasn't good for her to go without sleep.

"You may be right," Rose said. "I am sure if Frank were here, he'd tell me that I shouldn't wait up for him. But you're tired, too, aren't you? You ought not stay up either."

"I suppose not." By now it seemed clear that there was nothing Hester could do to help Mrs. Jamison or her lodgers. In the unlikely event that her assistance was needed, someone could simply wake her up.

Both women returned to their bedchambers, and Hester, at least, slept long past her usual waking time the next morning. When she awoke, she found a rather nasty surprise waiting for her. Neville Butler himself met her at the breakfast table. After the fire was extinguished, he'd spent the rest of the night at the vicarage, sleeping on the sofa in the parlor.

The meal was awkward, to say the least. Hester and Rose both studiously avoided talking to Mr. Butler. He initially tried to engage them in light conversation, but when he received no encouragement, he soon gave up. He finished his meal in a hurry, muttered something about sorting through the belongings he'd rescued from the fire, and left the room.

Afterwards, Frank pulled Hester aside to explain the situation. "I wanted to reassure you that Mr. Butler is not going to stay here one minute longer than necessary," he said firmly. "Later today, he'll move up to the castle, since they have extra bedrooms. He may leave some of his things here, but you won't need to see him after today."

Hester could only hope her brother-in-law was right.

Chapter Twelve

WALTER RETURNED TO Selwyn Castle, only to discover that Ingleton had gone up in flames during his absence. Well, more precisely, a single cottage in the village had burned down, along with a nearby shed. No lives were lost, but the widow Jamison's livelihood was destroyed.

And Neville Butler temporarily moved into Selwyn Castle, since he had nowhere else to stay for his last few days as Frank's assistant.

"Won't it be rather uncomfortable having him here, after the incident at the party?" Walter kept his voice down to a near whisper, not wanting to risk being overheard, even though the only person in the room other than him and Ivy was Viscount Elston, who lacked the vocabulary to repeat what they said.

"Yes, but it must have been even more uncomfortable for Hester yesterday. He stayed at the vicarage the day after the fire." Ivy set aside her knitting to give Walter her undivided attention.

Walter sucked in a sharp breath. "Good Lord, that man doesn't know when he's outstayed his welcome!"

How could Butler have the audacity to be a guest at the vicarage after insulting the vicar's younger sister? Men had been called out for less! Maybe clergymen weren't allowed to duel, Walter conceded, but he still didn't understand how Frank could offer shelter to the man who'd tried to compromise his sister.

That made it look as if Butler's actions were to be condoned, or at least ignored. Butler ought to have been publicly reprimanded, not treated as a houseguest!

Ivy studied his face and frowned. "I can't remember when I've seen you this angry, Walter. Is there something you're not telling us?"

He sighed and looked away, unwilling to admit his fascination with Lady Hester. His attention was caught by the sight of Lord Inglewhite's heir pulling books off a low bookshelf. "Should Robbie be doing that?"

"Oh dear!" Ivy sprang to her feet and hurried to rescue the books from her son. She tried to distract him with a coral rattle, but he threw it across the room and began to wail as only a toddler can.

That was Walter's cue to exit. "Would you like me to run up to the nursery to find one of his toys?" If he took long enough doing it, Robbie might calm down before he returned.

"No, thank you." Ivy scooped her son up. "He's probably hungry and tired. It's time to take him back to the nursery for a snack and a n-a-p."

Robbie abruptly stopped crying. "Snack?" he repeated, sounding hopeful. "Snack?"

Ivy smiled wryly at him. "Yes, it's snack time. Let's see what cook sent up for you!" She glanced back over her shoulder at Walter. "Butler will take his meals in his room rather than dining with us during his stay, so you needn't worry about encountering him at mealtime. I realize the two of you don't get along."

Walter snorted, though the door shutting behind Ivy probably prevented her from hearing it. "Don't get along" didn't even begin to describe how Walter felt about Neville Butler. It seemed increasingly likely that Butler was behind the falsified ledgers, but even if he wasn't a thief, he was a scoundrel through and through.

In the middle of his fuming, Walter realized there could be a bright side to Butler's unwanted presence at the castle. If nothing else, Walter might be able to keep a closer eye on Butler. Maybe he'd even have an opportunity to obtain a sample of Butler's handwriting.

Still thinking about the embezzlement case, Walter wandered into the library. Lord Inglewhite sat at his desk, spectacles perched on his nose, as he poured over a newspaper.

"I didn't know you wore spectacles," Walter observed.

"Hmm?" Inglewhite looked up. "Oh, Haworth. Yes, I had to get reading glasses last year. It was getting too hard to read fine print." He took the glasses off and rubbed his eyes. "Ivy thinks I should spare my eyes by letting my secretary handle more of my work. But back when I was a clergyman, I read and replied to all my correspondence myself. It doesn't seem right to have my secretary write all my letters just because I'm an earl now!"

Walter pounced on this segue. "Speaking of correspondence, do you happen to have any notes or letters from Mr. Butler? I'd like to take a look at his handwriting."

"His handwriting?" Inglewhite raised his brows. "May I ask why?"

Walter scanned the room, taking an especially hard look at the curtains framing the window seat. Today they were open, and there was no sign of an intruder. "Perhaps I had better tell you everything." He pulled up a chair and sat down. "It all began when the new matron at the Home noticed some discrepancies in the orphanage's account books." He went on to tell the entire story.

Inglewhite's eyes grew wider and wider as the story progressed. "And the board thought *you* were to blame for the embezzlement?"

"I don't think they thought it for very long." At least, he hoped not. "There really wasn't a plausible motive for me to steal from an orphanage. I have a perfectly adequate income."

"Unless you were hiding something," Inglewhite suggested. "Or being blackmailed."

Walter was so shocked, he leaned back in the chair, putting some distance between himself and his cousin-in-law. "Blackmailed? What would anyone even blackmail me for?" The worst wrongdoing he could remember was the time he tried to hide a pet rat in his room at Cambridge. He'd been caught when the rat, Nicodemus, escaped and scurried down the corridor. There were certainly no grounds for blackmail there!

"No, no," Inglewhite said soothingly. "I don't really think you are being blackmailed. I'm just saying it's the sort of thing that occasionally happens. Blackmail sometimes explains why a person who seems to be comfortably situated might have need of additional funds. But never mind that. Do you have any idea who *did* falsify the ledgers?"

"We had a few theories, but most of them have been ruled out by having a handwriting expert compare the writing in the ledger to the various suspects' handwriting."

"Ah." Inglewhite steepled his fingers together and nodded. "Hence your request for Mr. Butler's writing? He is one of the suspects?"

"One of the ones who has not yet been eliminated, yes." Neville Butler was number one on Walter's suspect list, but he kept that information to himself. He wasn't sure he could easily explain why he'd grown to dislike Butler so much. How much of it was envy over the ease with which Butler conversed with young ladies?

"I don't know that I do have anything in writing from him," Lord Inglewhite warned. "I never met the man until he started working as Frank's curate, you know, and I haven't had reason to correspond with him myself. I'll have my secretary look through my papers just in case there's something I've forgotten, but I can't promise anything."

"I appreciate your looking all the same." Walter felt unreasonably disappointed. He'd thought getting a piece of Butler's writing would be easy. Well, maybe it still would be. Frank must have notes or letters in Butler's hand.

"Speaking of Butler and charitable institutions, though. . ." Inglewhite left the sentence hanging, as if he expected Walter to intuit what he was hinting.

Walter had absolutely no idea where the earl was trying to take the conversation. "Yes? What about charitable organizations?"

"I don't know if you've ever met Sir Henry Skelton, but he's planning on turning one of his family properties into a hospital for sick children."

"Oh, yes! Based on the one in France?" When Inglewhite nodded, Walter added, "I haven't met Sir Henry, but I've heard a little bit about his proposal. It seems like a promising idea." Some of the children who'd arrive at the Haworth Home in poor health might have benefited from a hospital that specialized in children's illnesses.

Walter thought he knew what Inglewhite meant to say next, so he hurried to cut him off. "If you are looking for donors, I'm sorry to say that all of the funds from the Haworth charitable trust have already been dedicated to other projects. We just helped endow a school for freedmen in Barbados, so we're not able to take on any new philanthropic work."

"Oh, right, Ivy told me about that. I believe that was Mr. Robinson's idea, wasn't it?"

Walter nodded. Prior to the 1791 sugar boycott, Haworth & Haworth imported and processed sugarcane produced through slavery. The writings of William Fox convinced Frederic Haworth to stop buying sugarcane grown by slave labor and instead purchase "free-grown" sugar from other sources. Still, some of the Haworth wealth had come from slave labor. When Robinson married into the family, he suggested that supporting West Indian freedmen might somewhat counter-balance the company's previous complicity in slavery.

"Well, as it happens," Inglewhite continued, "I am not suggesting you invest *money* in the new hospital. You see, Sir Henry is looking for someone to manage the hospital. Given your interest in medicine, I thought you might consider applying for the position."

"Me?" Walter was surprised into a momentary silence. He'd never thought of taking a paid position outside of the family. On the contrary, he'd assumed he would eventually do as his father wanted and come home to manage Northcote Manor.

"I should clarify that the salary would be nominal," Inglewhite added. "I believe Sir Henry is hoping to find a man of some independent wealth to take on the position, so that he can use more of the money paying for physicians and nurses. That was the other reason I thought of you—you do not need to earn your bread."

"Quite so." Walter still felt overwhelmed by the suggestion. "I will have to think on this idea." He rose to his feet, intending to take his leave.

"Yes, yes. If you are interested, let me know and I can introduce you to Sir Henry."

Inglewhite stood up, too. "One last thing, Haworth."

"Yes?" Walter expected the earl to say something related to the family, some news about one of Walter's cousins, perhaps.

"Ivy and I are very grateful to you for rescuing Hester from what could have been a very unfortunate situation."

Walter drew in a breath, intending to deny any need for thanks, but Inglewhite earnestly held Walter's gaze with his eyes as he kept talking.

"You may not realize this, but the Bracknell family have been in the scandal sheets frequently over the last few years. I know that the Marchioness sent Hester here in the hopes that she'd stay out of trouble after some unpleasantness in London."

Unpleasantness? Walter frowned. "I hadn't heard about any unpleasantness." He thought Lady Hester had come to Ingleton simply because Rose needed her assistance. Women did often travel to attend their relatives' confinements. There was nothing unusual about that.

"No, you wouldn't have," Inglewhite agreed. "The Bracknells are trying to keep it under wraps. I will only say that Lady Hester has already been caught in a situation that damaged her good name. To be caught again—well, I don't know if she could have recovered from a second scandal. So, we very much appreciate your intervention."

"I did not do it to avoid scandal. I merely wanted to help a lady in distress." The moment the words left his mouth, Walter second-guessed them. He sounded pretentious, didn't he? As if he thought he were a modern-day Sir Lancelot! Embarrassed, he stared down at the carpet, as if examining his boots for defects.

"Whatever your motives, we appreciate your quick intervention. I would hate to see *any* young woman forced into matrimony with such a rogue, but the Bracknells have already had more than their share of trouble." For a moment, Lord Inglewhite looked distinctly sad, though he set his private sorrow aside to bid Walter goodbye.

More than their share of trouble. As he left the library, intending to return to his room, Walter turned those words over in his mind, wondering what exactly had happened to Lady Hester in London. He knew that the eldest Bracknell son, Lord Crowthorne, had fled England a couple of years ago under a cloud of disgrace, but he knew no more than the bare facts of the case. Did the Bracknells go looking for trouble, or did it find them?

One his way upstairs, he passed Neville Butler heading down. When the curate silently nodded a greeting, Walter returned the nod. He said nothing to Butler, but his mind raced. If Butler was heading downstairs, that meant he wasn't in his guestroom. In his absence, there'd be nothing to stop Walter from taking a quick look around Butler's room.

When he reached the corridor leading into the wing of guest rooms, Walter picked up his pace. He had no idea where Butler was going or what he intended to do. He couldn't count on having a long time to search the room. He'd have to restrict himself to a quick peek around the room and hope he got well away from the room before Butler returned.

Fortune favored Walter: Butler's bedroom door was unlocked, and there were no maids tidying up the room, as he'd half feared. On the other hand, there really wasn't much of anything in the room. He found a few smoky garments hanging in the wardrobe; a Bible and prayerbook on the nightstand next to the bed; and a small metal box that rattled when Walter shook it. It sounded like it contained only coins.

Walter scanned the room one more time, but he couldn't see any paperwork at all. He picked up both the Bible and the Book of Common Prayer and flipped through them, thinking there might be a note stuck between pages to serve as a bookmark. Nothing! Had all Butler's notes and records gone up in flames?

As he turned to leave, Walter thought of one last possibility. Feeling foolish in the extreme, he squatted down beside the bed and peered beneath. Success! Something blocked the light streaming in from the other side. He reached a hand through and encountered leather—a satchel or bag, perhaps.

Heart pounding, he dragged it out. Yes, it was a leather satchel, the sort sometimes carried by schoolboys. Walter opened it and began to sort through the contents. It primarily contained letters, none of which seemed to be signed with Butler's name. Well, of course not! Naturally, the correspondence Butler kept would be letters to him from other people, not letters *from* him.

Walter's heart sank as he realized that even this find looked like a dead end. He half-heartedly flipped through the letters, just in case there was a scrap of Walter's writing somewhere.

He stopped flipping when a familiar name caught his eye. He pulled a thin piece of notepaper out so he could see it more clearly. Yes, he'd correctly read the name "Bracknell," though he struggled to make out the surrounding words. He folded the case shut, rose to his feet, and stepped closer to the window, hoping the afternoon sunlight would make the writing more legible.

"*. . . the Bracknell family is particularly vulnerable now,*" the letter said, "*in the wake of L.'s attempt to blackmail C. He still has the stolen letters and is prepared to use them if C. ever returns from America.*"

Walter would have kept reading, but the sound of a nearby

door clicking shut reminded him that there were other people in the house. He couldn't allow himself to be caught searching Butler's things! He folded the letter up and tucked it into his waistcoat pocket. Then he shoved the satchel back under the bed, doing his best to leave it exactly where he'd found it. He didn't want to leave any signs that he'd been here.

Before he left, he glanced around the room to see if he'd left anything out of order. Was the stack of books on the nightstand crooked? He hastily straightened it, although he could not remember for sure what it looked like before he searched the books. He could only hope that any disturbance in the room would be insignificant enough to go unnoticed.

Feeling rather foolish, Walter rested an ear against the door, listening for sounds from the corridor. When he heard nothing, he slipped out the door, shut it quietly, and hurried back towards the staircase.

On the way down the staircase, he ran into Neville Butler again. Quite literally this time, as their arms bumped in passing.

"My apologies, Mr. Haworth. I did not mean to intrude on you." Butler sketched a mocking bow.

Walter bit back the angry retort he wanted to make. This was no time to provoke Butler! He'd left Butler's guestroom not a moment too soon. A minute later, and Walter might've been the one caught in wrongdoing.

He pasted a contrite smile on his face. "No need to apologize," he replied. "I'm as much in the wrong as you are. I ought to've watched where I was going. I'll keep my eyes open in the future."

"As will I." Butler's lopsided smile looked more like a sneer. "I'll watch out for you, Haworth. You can be sure of that." He inclined his head and hurried up the stairs.

Walter stared after him. That sounded more like a threat than like a promise. What, exactly, would Butler be on the watch for? Could he have figured out that Walter was investigating him? If so, Walter's task had just gotten even more difficult.

Chapter Thirteen

HESTER DID NOT mean to eavesdrop on Mr. Haworth a second time. She no longer had a reason to spy on him. Though she remained deeply curious about the conversation she'd overheard between him and Lady Inglewhite, she no longer believed he was up to anything illegal or immoral. Nor did she fear him dragging Frank into any kind of trouble from which he might need rescuing.

Maybe it would be more accurate to say that she didn't want to believe ill of Mr. Haworth, not after he'd single-handedly rescued her from Neville Butler. Her first impressions of Mr. Haworth might have been as wrong as her first impressions of Mr. Butler. She'd learned that a solicitor could sometimes behave in a more gentlemanly way than a clergyman.

No, she would go farther than that. Walter Haworth *was* a gentleman, regardless of how he earned his living. Neville Butler clearly was not. Now she wondered how Mr. Butler had fooled people into ordaining him as a clergyman, or how he'd fooled Frank into thinking he would make an acceptable curate. Surely such villainy ought to be detectable? It didn't seem right that so unprincipled a man could be mistaken for a devout son of the church.

Life, Hester was beginning to realize, was somewhat more complicated than she'd ever been told.

In any case, she'd come down to the parlor intending to look for a book Rose had mislaid. It took forever for her to find it, and when she did, she spied it at the very top of a bookcase. The third volume of *Frankenstein* leaned against a stack of what looked like bound sermons. It would have been easy to grab the book if she'd been a few inches taller, but as it was, it lay beyond her reach.

A month ago, Hester would have rung for a servant to retrieve the book for her. Back then, it wouldn't have occurred to her to wonder how a maid shorter than herself could reach the book, or whether it would be necessary to bring a stepstool into the room. She would have simply assumed that it was a servant's job to figure out how to retrieve the book.

By now, though, she knew that the vicarage servants were too busy with their own work to do things she could just as easily do herself. So, Hester dragged a lightweight armchair over to the bookcase, stood on the chair, and reached for the book. Success!

But in the next moment, her success turned into disaster. She got hold of the book she wanted, yes, but she must have jostled the stack of bound sermons next to it. The sermons toppled over with a spectacular crash, falling right off the bookshelf. To be precise, they fell behind the enormous wing chair in the corner of the room. Once again, they lay beyond her reach.

Hester put the volume of *Frankenstein* on the nearest tea table so she wouldn't lose track of it. Then she scrambled behind the wing chair to pick up the sermons, praying that no one walked into the room and caught her behaving with so little dignity.

To her surprise, the fallen books weren't the only things hiding behind the chair. She also found a round leather ball, a cricket ball, she thought. How on earth had *that* gotten here? She couldn't imagine anyone trying to play cricket indoors, especially in a room this small.

Hester was still puzzling over the cricket ball when the door opened and two people walked into the room. She ought to have announced her presence immediately, but she was too embarrassed at the prospect of being caught crouching behind the chair to call attention to herself. She made herself as small as possible and prayed that she wouldn't be stuck there for long.

"I seem to have disposed of most of the letters I exchanged with Neville when I arranged for him to work here. Probably turned them into spills for lighting candles." Frank's voice was immediately recognizable. "There was no reason to keep them. But I think I have a note in his handwriting here. Ah! Yes, I was using it as a bookmark. Will that do?"

"I hope so." Mr. Haworth sounded doubtful. "It's a good example of his signature, but the message itself isn't exceedingly long. I think Mr. Hunt was hoping for a long letter. He particularly wanted something with numerals as well as letters, so he could compare the numbers in Butler's writing to the numbers in the ledger."

"I doubt I have anything with numbers," Frank confessed, "but I'll keep my eyes open. You say it's a case of embezzlement?"

"Yes. But we don't know for certain that Butler's the guilty party. He's only one of the suspects! And I must ask you not to repeat any of what I've said to you on the subject. Apart from telling Rose, I mean. I don't suppose you need to keep it a secret from her."

Frank chuckled softly. "I don't suppose I *can* keep a secret from her! Somehow, she can always tell when there's something I'm trying to conceal. Makes it hard to hide gifts or plan surprises, I can tell you!"

"Now that does not surprise me one bit." A laugh lurked behind Mr. Haworth's words. "When we were children, she was always particularly good at finding out people's secrets. She was especially good at interpreting Ivy's expressions, too." He continued talking as the men exited the room, leaving Hester alone to grapple with what she'd just learned.

Goodness. Neville Butler must be even more evil than she'd imagined! He'd made it obvious that he was a man of few principles, but she hadn't expected him to commit a crime like embezzlement. She rather thought that might be a hanging crime, depending on how much money was stolen. But she couldn't be certain. It wasn't as if she'd ever had to memorize the Bloody Code.

Mr. Haworth had said they did not know for certain that Mr. Butler was the embezzler. But Butler's guilt would certainly fit with everything Hester had learned about him over the last month. He was on the hunt for an heiress or a woman whose family could materially advance his career, and he was willing to behave dishonorably in order to achieve his goal. That suggested that he either wanted or needed money rather badly. She could readily believe he might steal to get it.

And now those investigating the crime needed a piece of his handwriting? Something with numbers on it? The numbers would be the challenge, she suspected. A letter from Mr. Butler might have the date on it, but she had no idea whether that would be adequate.

By now, Rose must wonder what had happened to Hester. She picked up *Frankenstein* and hurried out to the garden. She found Rose resting in the shade of a beech tree, her feet propped up on a chair.

"Sorry to keep you waiting!" Hester called. "It took me forever to find it." She made no mention of her accidental eavesdropping.

"I thought maybe you'd absconded with it," Rose joked, "and intended to read it before I had a chance."

Hester scrunched up her face. "*Frankenstein* isn't exactly my favorite." She'd found the first volume so disgusting that she hadn't bothered to read further. She handed the book over with a feigned shudder.

"Yes, volumes of poetry are more to your taste," Rose agreed. "We all know that. What's the name of that poet you like?"

"Maria Grammar." Hester froze as she remembered something about Grammar's poetry. When Butler gave her the new book of Grammar's poems, he'd tucked a note into it, hadn't he? A note covered with page numbers of his supposed favorite poems. *Numbers!*

"Is something wrong, Hetty?" Rose peered up at her, squinting her eyes against the sun.

"Nothing's wrong! I just remembered something I needed to look up. I mean, look for. I mean, I need to go look at something I just remembered." She clamped her mouth shut in a desperate attempt to end her senseless babbling. "Do you mind if I don't read out here after all?"

Rose waved her away. "I am perfectly fine out here on my own. Go look for whatever-it-is before you forget it again."

That seemed like such good advice that Hester practically ran up the stairs to her room. The book of poems sat on a shelf in the corner of the room. She opened it up, praying she hadn't discarded the note. But her luck held: she had used it as a bookmark, and it was still there.

She pulled it out and scanned it. Yes, as she'd remembered, there was a list of poems Butler recommended, complete with page numbers. Better still, between those different page numbers she found all the numerals from 1 to 9. She had no idea whether this would be enough for Mr. Haworth's purposes, but surely it would help a little! Now all she had to do was find the opportunity to give it to him. . . and to think of an explanation for how she knew that he needed it.

On Friday, Frank left town to visit an ailing friend from university, Mr. Montgomery. To say that he was nervous about being apart from Rose would be the understatement of the decade. He arranged for her medical attendant to examine her before he left, though Rose swore up and down that she was perfectly fine and had no reason to think she was about to go into labor.

As if that were not enough, he arranged for Lady Inglewhite to visit every day of his absence. "I would feel better if I knew someone was checking in regularly," he explained.

"But I'm already here to look after Rose!" Hester protested. Wasn't that the whole point of her staying at the vicarage? She was supposed to make herself useful during her sister-in-law's confinement!

"Yes," he said impatiently, "but you've never had a baby, and Ivy has. She might know if something was wrong."

Since Hester couldn't argue with that, she held her tongue. When she caught Rose's gaze, Rose lifted her eyes and smiled wryly at her. Evidently, she thought Frank worried o'er much, too.

But, as it turned out, Frank's anxiety worked in Hester's favor. On Saturday morning, Lady Inglewhite called on Rose, and she brought Mr. Haworth with her. This was Hester's chance to pass him the note. Since the callers were relatives rather than mere acquaintances, she knew they'd likely stay longer than the standard half hour formal call.

Hester eagerly waited for a chance to pass the note to Mr. Haworth. She had imagined that something might call Rose and Lady Inglewhite out of the room for a moment, leaving her free to deliver the note and a quick explanation. She'd forgotten that Rose was supposed to stay reclined on the sofa as much as possible, with her feet elevated.

If Mr. Haworth had chosen to sit in a distant corner of the parlor, Hester might've tried to slip the note to him anyway. But, not surprisingly, he'd taken a chair near the sofa so he could talk to Rose. There was simply no opportunity to talk to him alone.

In desperation, Hester sent Mr. Haworth a "significant look". She caught his eye, stared at him, then shifted her gaze to the chair next to hers, trying to silently signal that she wanted him to move across the room and sit beside her. He responded only by furrowing his brow in confusion.

Rose noticed the look, but misinterpreted it. "Hester, is that seat too hard? I believe the armchair in the corner has more padding. You might find it more comfortable."

"Oh no," Hester replied. "I was just comparing the different shades of red. I believe this chair is prettier." She felt clever for having invented so plausible an explanation on the spur of the moment, but she was no closer to passing the note to Mr. Haworth.

She had to give up when Lady Inglewhite rose to her feet, signaling an end to the visit. The chance for a tête-à-tête never materialized. Hester would have to find a different opportunity to give Mr. Haworth the note. And if she couldn't find an opportunity, she would make one.

Chapter Fourteen

T HE MONDAY AFTER the fire, Walter devoted the afternoon to answering letters. Since Inglewhite used the library for his work, Walter took over the green salon. Ivy assured him that no one used the room during Robbie's afternoon nap. Its first story location meant that it was in a quieter part of the castle. The distant sound of birdsong from the garden provided a soothing backdrop for his work.

Which made it all the more startling when the butler, Gibson, scratched at the door. Before Walter could answer, Gibson entered the room bearing a calling card.

"Hmm?" Walter looked up and blinked. He'd spent nearly an hour focusing on crossed-over letters, and it took a moment for his eyes to adjust.

"Lady Hester Bracknell to see you, sir," Gibson informed him.

"To see *me*?" Walter repeated, startled. Proper young ladies did not call on young gentlemen. Not even if their older brothers were married to the gentlemen's cousins. That was a tenuous connection, at best.

"Yes, sir. She says there is something she wishes to discuss with you. Privately." Gibson's face conveyed stern, silent disapproval as only a well-trained butler can.

"Very well. You may show her in." He put his quill back in

the penholder and set aside the letter he'd been drafting.

He rose to his feet as Lady Hester walked into the room. She shut the door behind her, leaving them alone in the room. Walter wanted to protest that this was all most irregular. They ought not be in a room alone! But she knew the rules as well as he did, if not better. She must have a reason for breaking them.

Lady Hester came to a stop some two yards away from him. "Thank you for meeting me, Mr. Haworth. You are probably surprised to see me."

"Yes," he admitted, "I am." If anything, he would have expected Lady Hester to be leery of being in a room alone with a man, after her experience with Neville Butler. "Is there some way in which I can help you?"

She cleared her throat. "Actually, I believe there may be a way I can help *you*." She opened her reticule and pulled out a piece of paper, folded into thirds. "But first, I have a bit of a confession to make." She lowered her eyes, looking unexpectedly bashful.

"Oh?" Walter hoped his voice sounded encouraging and non-judgmental, but he mostly just felt confused. What could she possibly need to confess? "Would this be easier if you sat down?"

"Ah, maybe." Lady Hester sat on the least-comfortable looking chair in the room. She sat with her hands neatly folded, her feet flat on the floor, and her back not touching the chair back. She looked as prim as the deportment instructor at a girl's finishing school.

Lady Hester drew a deep breath and announced, "I am afraid that the other day, I happened to overhear a conversation between you and my brother that I ought not have heard."

Conversation? Walter rifled through his memories, trying to recall any conversations with Frank that Lady Hester could have overheard. The last time he'd seen her brother had been on Friday... *oh.* He caught his breath sharply as he remembered what they'd talked about that day.

"You probably have many questions—" he began to say, but

she interrupted him with a raised hand and a shake of her head.

"It sounds as if what I heard was supposed to be kept secret, so I will not ask any questions. But I did wonder if you could use a note in Mr. Butler's writing, one that includes numbers as well as letters."

A jolt of excitement set Walter's heart skipping. He leaned forward eagerly. "You have a note from him? And you're sure it's his writing?" It wouldn't do to mistakenly use someone else's writing for comparison.

"Very certain. He put this note in a book he gave me." Pale pink tinted her cheeks, but she handed the note to Walter without further comment.

Yes, the note was signed "Neville Butler," and as Lady Hester had promised, it included numerals as well as letters. Page numbers, Walter saw, listing Butler's supposedly favorite poems by Miss Grammar.

"Do the two of you often talk about poetry, then?" He spoke without thinking, and felt immediately embarrassed. It was none of his business who Lady Hester spoke to or what she discussed!

Though if they'd been in the habit of corresponding with each other about books, that might account for Butler's belief that Lady Hester would accept his offer. An unmarried lady was not supposed to exchange letters with an unmarried gentleman unless the two of them were betrothed.

"I wouldn't say often." Lady Hester sounded cross. "I talked about the work of Miss Grammar once or twice, and he bought me a copy of her newest book of poetry." She stared down at her own hands. "I wasn't certain, then, whether he meant it in the light of a courtship present, though in hindsight I wish I'd simply rejected the book. I ought not have accepted a gift from him. It may have given him. . . encouragement."

"No amount of encouragement justifies a man in trying to compromise a woman in order to make her marry him." There were simply some things a gentleman should never do!

Thinking of propriety and compromise, though, reminded

Walter that he'd been alone in a room with Lady Hester for too long. He glanced nervously at the closed door, then back at her. "I thank you for this note," he began, "but—"

The door swung open to reveal the very last person Walter wanted to see: Neville Butler himself. How long had he been outside the door? Had he overheard any of the conversation? Walter prayed that even if Butler had overhead anything, he would be unable to figure out why Walter wanted a sample of his handwriting.

Butler looked from Walter to Lady Hester and raised his eyebrows. "Am I interrupting something? My apologies. I had a question for Mr. Haworth, but I can return when you've finished your *private* conversation." In his sneering mouth, otherwise innocuous words became laden with innuendo.

"Actually, I was just about to leave. Thank you, Mr. Haworth, for your sage advice." Lady Hester rose from her chair, as elegant and cool as she had ever been. One would never have been able to tell from her face that only a few minutes ago she'd been blushing as she confessed to overhearing a private conversation.

"You are very welcome, my lady," Walter replied.

Butler held the door open for her, and then stepped into the room. He took a seat without having been invited to do so and leaned back in the chair, as if prepared for a comfortable chat. Only the obnoxiously knowing smirk on his face indicated that he wasn't here for a pleasant social visit.

Walter clenched his hands into fists, wishing he could wipe the smirk off Butler's face. Instead, he asked, "Was there something I could help you with, Mr. Butler?" Unfortunately, Walter lacked Lady Hester's acting ability. His irritation seeped into his voice.

Butler's smile deepened in response, as if Walter's anger amused him. "I wanted to have a word with you about the incident at Lady Hester's birthday party."

Walter quietly seethed. How could Butler mention that incident so casually? He had nearly ruined the life of a genteel young lady. Though rarely a violent man, Walter wrestled with the desire to plant the scoundrel a facer.

A few deep breaths calmed him enough to speak. "What exactly do you wish to say about that incident?"

"I hope we are in agreement that there is no need to speak about that night to anyone else. Though merely a misunderstanding, it was understandably painful to Lady Hester, and I believe it would be in her best interest not to worry the rest of her family with the details. Wouldn't you agree?" Butler's smile would have appeared benevolent if Walter hadn't known the truth about his attempted coercion.

Walter stared at the curate, hating his smug smile, his air of assurance, and the fashionable tie of his cravat. If Butler was so desperate for money, how did he afford such fashionable clothing? Probably, Walter concluded, Butler's expensive taste in menswear accounted for his need to marry well.

"I don't think we are in agreement on this matter." Walter spoke slowly, choosing each word carefully. "If you ask me, Lord and Lady Reading have a right to know about your attempt to compromise their daughter. In fact, you're fortunate not to have been called out for your actions."

Butler chuckled softly, though there was no real mirth in the sound. "And who would challenge me to a duel? Lord Reading is an invalid who rarely leaves home, Lord Francis is a man of the cloth, and I doubt any gentleman would accept a challenge from Lord Crowthorne after the way he fled England in disgrace."

Why *had* Lord Crowthorne fled the country? Walter pushed the question aside. It wasn't important now. What was important was making it clear to Neville Butler that Lady Hester was not without friends.

"I believe you've forgotten that Lady Hester has other family members," Walter pointed out. "Her cousin is married to the Earl of Inglewhite, after all." Not that Inglewhite would ever agree to a dawn meeting. "Her parents have not left her unprotected."

To Walter's surprise, Butler replied with a snort. "Cousin? You mean the previous marquis's by-blow? She did well for herself in snagging a prime catch like Inglewhite, but she doesn't have enough social credit to spare any for Lady Hester."

Walter gritted his teeth and clenched his fists so tightly that his fingernails dug into his skin. "Perhaps you've forgotten that Lady Inglewhite is also *my* cousin, and that you are a guest in her home. I must ask you not to disparage her in my presence."

Once again, Butler smirked at him. He seemed pleased to have rattled Walter. "My apologies, Mr. Haworth. I intended no offense. I'm sure that in their own social circles, the Haworths are just as proud of their name and reputation as any aristocrat could be. But I fear that allying themselves with the Bracknell family will not add to their credit the way they may have hoped."

Walter's frown deepened. He wanted to argue that Butler had clearly misunderstood the situation. Rose's marriage to Lord Francis Bracknell had been a love match, as ought to be obvious to anyone who'd observed the two of them together. And there weren't any other Haworths attempting to "ally themselves" with the Bracknells, or any other aristocrats, for that matter!

Unless Butler thought Walter was courting Lady Hester? Walter drew in a sharp breath as he realized that probably was what Butler imagined. The curate had just interrupted Walter in a private conversation with Lady Hester. From the outside, that might very well look more like courtship, or even seduction, than the collaboration it really was.

Walter longed to angrily protest that he, unlike Butler, was not in the market for an aristocratic bride. He wasn't looking for a wife at all! And if he *had* been on the hunt for a bride, he would've looked for her among his own circle of acquaintances. Between his father's old business contacts and the people Walter met through managing the Haworth philanthropies, he had plenty of social connections of his own. He had no need to insinuate himself into a noble family.

Even so, Walter did his best to control his anger. "I think you have misunderstood the situation. Lady Hester and I were merely discussing a mutual acquaintance."

Butler raised his eyebrows. "If you so say." That damnable mocking smirk twisted the corner of his mouth up again. "So, are we in agreement that you will not tell anyone about my failed proposal last week?"

Walter's mouth fell ajar. Failed proposal? Was *that* what he called it? "No," Walter replied. "I will not agree to that. I will pass that information on to anyone whom I believe has a right to know it." For instance, Butler's future employers, or any young ladies who had the misfortune to become the object of his unwanted attentions.

The smile fell away from Butler's face. "That's how you want to play this, is it? Noted. I wish you the best of luck, Mr. Haworth."

Butler rose to his feet, turned on his heel, and exited the room, leaving Walter with a cold, sick feeling of anxiety. He had no idea what Butler meant, but he knew whatever he had in mind for Walter, it wouldn't be good.

❦

Chapter Fifteen

F RANK DID NOT come back on Monday or Tuesday, as originally planned. Instead, he sent a letter saying that Montgomery's health had worsened; the end was approaching faster than anticipated. The poor man had no family nearby, so Frank planned to stay on hand to comfort and to minister to his friend in his last days.

No one liked this delay. Though Rose felt sorry for poor Mr. Montgomery, she thought it vastly unfair that her husband should be called out of town when her expected date of confinement was so close. Meanwhile, Neville Butler lingered in Ingleton during Frank's absence, covering the religious services at St. John's. Hester waited anxiously for Butler's next move, certain that he had not given up the fight.

During the last week of June, summer warmth blanketed the town, and children played on the green late into the long summer evenings. Rose's due date came and went, taking with it her usually cheerful disposition. She grumbled about her discomfort, complained about the warm weather, and wondered whether her baby would ever arrive.

Rose experienced occasional contractions, but they stayed a good five or ten minutes apart, never coming closer together. Her doctor called it "false labor" and warned her that true labor might still be weeks away. Rose was not best pleased by this information.

In the meantime, the nursery stood ready and waiting for the baby, and Rose interviewed and hired a monthly nurse who moved into the already-crowded servants' quarters so she'd be on hand for labor and delivery.

On Wednesday, the mercury in the thermometer climbed to its highest yet. Hester and Rose lounged in the garden, hoping to catch a breeze. At first, Rose fanned herself and groused about the heat. Then she fell silent, lay down her fan, and closed her eyes, apparently lulled to sleep.

Hester kept moving her chair in an attempt to find the best shade. The warmth did not bother Hester, but the bright afternoon light exacerbated the headache she'd been nursing all day. Left to herself, she would have preferred to rest indoors, with the curtains drawn against the light. She'd only come out to the garden to keep Rose company.

One of the housemaids stepped out of the house, shading her eyes against the light. "Lady Hester? Mr. Haworth has called and wishes to speak to you."

Hester looked up from her sewing. Rose opened her eyes, apparently not asleep after all. "To see both of us, or just Hester?" she clarified.

The nervous maid twisted her apron. "He only said Lady Hester, ma'am."

Hester exchanged a puzzled look with Rose. It must be something to do with Neville Butler, Hester guessed. Had Butler made some new threat? What more could he do than he'd already done? She wasn't sure she wanted to know. Just thinking of the possibilities made her palms sweat.

"I will meet him," she told the maid. "He is in the parlor, I presume?"

"Yes, ma'am."

"Thank you, Daisy. You may tell him that I will be there in a minute. And please fetch a pot of tea for us, if you will."

While the maid hurried to pass on the message, Hester took a moment to tidy her wind-blown hair and brush off her gown. She wished she had a looking glass on hand, but she did not want to go all the way to her room first. That would make it look as if she were deeply concerned about her appearance, which of course was not true. There was no need to make a special effort for Mr. Haworth.

Hester drew a deep breath and stepped back into the house. After the bright light of the sun-drenched garden, the corridor seemed downright Stygian. Each step she took sounded unnaturally loud, leaving her feeling like an iron-shod draft horse.

She found Walter Haworth in the parlor, pacing back and forth in front of the window. He turned towards her the moment the door opened. The slanting afternoon sunlight gilded his hair and glinted off his spectacles, making him look unexpectedly prepossessing.

He ceased his pacing and stood before her. "Lady Hester, thank you so much for meeting with me today! I promise not to take up too much of your time." His deep voice, sounding both firm and unflappable, could have reassured a herd of skittish deer.

"You are very welcome." Though his confidence reassured her, Hester still spoke more softly than usual, because finding the right words had become surprisingly difficult. "Won't you have a seat, Mr. Haworth?"

She herself sat on what she knew to be hardest, least comfortable chair in the room. She needed the support of the straight back, because something fluttered in her stomach, making her feel oddly shaky.

Strangely, Hester felt more nervous around Mr. Haworth now than she had when they first met, weeks ago. She could not imagine why that would be the case. By now, he'd proven himself to be a perfect gentleman in nature, if not by birth.

"Thank you," he repeated. "I would not have troubled you with this matter, if your brother were available. However, I am leaving town tomorrow and I doubt he will return in time for me to speak to him. I thought it best to speak to at least one member of the Bracknell family."

Hester's mouth went dry. She swallowed heavily, wishing she had a cup of tea. Ought she to ring for tea? "What matter do you speak of?" His solemn expression suggested it must be bad news of one sort or another.

Mr. Haworth took off his glasses, pulled out a handkerchief, and polished the lenses. "This is very awkward to explain. As you know, I needed a sample of Mr. Butler's writing in order to investigate some criminal activity." He put his spectacles back on and looked up with a little more confidence. "By the way, I must thank you again for giving me that note about the poems. It looks perfect for our purposes. In fact, I am on the way to Bristol to give the paper to Mr. Hunt, the handwriting expert assisting with this case."

"You are very welcome," Hester assured him. "I am glad to have been of service." She glanced at the door, realizing that she'd let it fall closed, rather than propping it open for the sake of propriety. If anyone walked in on them, what would they think? "Was that all you had to say?"

"No." He cleared his voice, looking as nervous as Hester felt. "As I was saying, I needed a piece of Butler's writing. Before you gave me that excellent sample, I—well, I must confess that I searched Mr. Butler's guestroom in the hopes of finding a useable piece of writing." The tips of his ears turned bright red.

Hester blinked. "Oh my," she said, because some response seemed to be necessary. She didn't think it would be helpful to ask, "Weren't you ashamed of snooping through his personal effects?" or "What has this to do with me?" even though she wondered about both questions.

"I did not find what I wanted." Mr. Haworth drew a deep breath and continued, although he kept looking away from Hester. He stared out the window, as if there were something positively riveting about the summer day. "But I found a letter that I thought you—or your brother—might be interested in. You see, it mentions the Bracknell family by name. And it refers explicitly to you."

"It does?" Hester spoke more sharply than she'd intended. He had her full attention now.

Mr. Haworth pulled a folded letter out of his pocket. "Yes. You can see right here, the paragraph beginning 'Be sure.' I circled the relevant part with a pencil."

He handed her the letter, and she peered down at it. The circled text made the selected passage easy for her to find. Unfortunately, it did not make for easy reading.

Be sure to let me know how your heiress trap works. You've chosen a good target. The Bracknell family is particularly vulnerable now, thanks to L. having blackmailed C two or three years ago. The plan failed when C. fled the country, but L. assures me that he still has the stolen letters and is prepared to use them if C. ever returns. I suspect Reading will agree to well-nigh anything to keep the family name from being further sullied.

A sour taste filled Hester's mouth. She had no idea who L. was, but C. must be her brother, Lord Crowthorne. At a winter house party two and a half years ago, he had stolen a fortune's worth of jewelry, only to lose the jewels when a Bow Street Runner found them. Over and over in her head, she wondered: blackmailed for *what*? What could Crowthorne have done that was so terrible he'd steal his own mother's jewelry to silence his blackmailer?

The letter began to shake as her hands trembled. She handed the paper back to Mr. Haworth and clasped her hands together, hoping to still the tremor.

"Yes, I know. I have no idea whether that is true; you might know better than I." He looked at her expectantly.

She shook her head. "In the note he left for my mother, Crowthorne said only that he needed the money to cover debts of honor. That was all the reason he gave us." Everyone had assumed that "debts of honor" meant gambling debts, though they'd not previously realized he had a gaming habit.

Crowthorne had only written home once since then, to announce that he'd arrived safely in America. He hadn't even given them an address at which they might contact him. He'd told them not to worry, but Hester knew her mother worried her heart out, anyway. How could she not? As for their father, well, the Marquis simply refused to discuss his eldest son.

"I don't know if this has occurred to you," Mr. Haworth said diffidently, "but if you ever needed evidence of Mr. Butler's scheme to compromise you, this might help make your case."

"Oh. I hadn't thought of that." All her attention had been consumed by the references to her older brother. "I don't suppose there's any way to find out who this L. person is?"

Mr. Haworth hesitated. "Mr. Butler might be able to tell us that, but I rather doubt that he would be willing to talk."

Hester nodded, since she'd expected that. "May I keep this letter? I would like to show it to Frank when he comes home."

She hoped he'd know what, if anything, they should do with this information. Hester herself had no idea whether her parents should be informed about the blackmail. If there was nothing that could be done to help Crowthorne, there might be no point in revealing the contents of the letter.

"Of course!" Mr. Haworth smiled crookedly. "I only wish there was more I could do to help you, my lady. It is most unfair that your family has been targeted in this way."

Hester returned his smile. "You have been immensely helpful already," she assured him. "I am in your debt."

At that moment, Daisy returned, bearing a heavily laden tea tray. Hester did her best to set aside all her questions so she could play hostess. "Can I offer you any refreshments?"

Mr. Haworth shook his head and rose to his feet. "I thank you, no. I had best return to the castle and ready my things for tomorrow's journey."

"Then I must wish you safe travels." She offered him her hand in farewell.

He took her hand, squeezed it gently, then bowed a farewell to her. She stared after him a moment before sitting down to brew the tea. She needed liquid sustenance after the revelation about Crowthorne, and she hoped the homely business of drinking tea would restore her composure.

Rose returned from the garden to take tea with her. When she entered the room, she shot a curious look at Hester, but something about Hester's face must have dissuaded her from asking any questions about the encounter with Walter Haworth.

Instead, she settled herself comfortably on the sofa, then asked, "Did you hurt your hand?"

"Hmm? What do you mean?" Hester stared blankly at Rose. At the moment, the only pain she felt was the dull ache of her fading megrim.

"You keep rubbing your right hand," Rose explained. "I thought you must have somehow injured it. Did you burn it on the teapot?"

"Oh!" Hester glanced down at her hand. She had been cradling it in her left hand without realizing it. "No. Um. Not exactly. Something just irritated it."

Irritated was not really the right word, but even if Hester had known the correct word, she would've been too embarrassed to say it. Ever since Walter Haworth squeezed her hand, she'd been hyperaware of it, as if his touch haunted her.

She wasn't starting to fancy Mr. Haworth, was she? Oh, how foolish! She had just escaped a potentially scandalous situation with Mr. Butler. She could not afford to develop a *tendre* for a man whom her parents would undoubtedly consider ineligible. That way lay nothing but heartache!

Chapter Sixteen

W ALTER RUBBED HIS palm against the side of his leg, as if he could scratch off the memory of Lady Hester's hand in his. His heart thumped erratically. What was *that* about? He was not sure which confused him more: Lady Hester's changed demeanor, or his reaction to it.

He had once thought Lady Hester cold, proud, and supercilious. But today, she'd smiled at him as if she meant it. As if she were a perfectly normal girl who was genuinely grateful for his help, rather than a queen graciously receiving assistance she thought was her due.

Stranger still, the distant reserve that had characterized her in the past had somehow changed to a charming bashfulness. In another girl, he might have thought that was coyness, but there'd been an artless air about her blushes and hesitations that made them seem genuine.

Good Lord, Walter thought. This was ridiculous! It was time to face facts: he had, perhaps, become a little smitten with the visitor at the vicarage. That was only natural, he supposed. Lady Hester was a lovely, cultured young woman. Any man might admire such a lady.

What embarrassed him beyond words, though, was that he'd started imagining signs that she might return his interest. It was not very likely that the daughter of a marquis would entertain warm sentiments towards a solicitor born from a *nouveau riche* family. Whatever indications of interest he thought he saw were undoubtedly maggots born of wishful thinking. Probably just as well that he was leaving Ingleton for a time!

Two tasks drew Walter out of Ingleton. The first was passing the handwritten note to Ernest, who would see that his handwriting expert got a chance to look at it. Walter could have relied on the mail to deliver it, except that his second errand took him to Northcote Manor, not far south of Bristol. Walter's father had been asking to see him for months, and Walter could no longer put off a visit, much as he might want to do so.

June went out in a series of bright days, the green of the fields and the blue of the sky undimmed by clouds or rain. In some fields, haymaking continued; in others, golden wheat fields promised a rich harvest. Maybe food would be plentiful this winter.

At least the tenants on Haworth land all seemed to be thriving. Walter, tired of riding in a carriage all day, sent the post chaise on ahead of him so he could walk the last two or three miles on the way home. He stopped at Apple Hill farm to chat with Mr. Weston, whose orchards were the pride of the county.

"Your father'll be glad to see you, Mr. Haworth," the farmer said. The wink that accompanied this prediction embarrassed Walter. He hated the way everyone near the Manor seemed to know that he and his father did not get along.

"I've been busy," Walter said. It sounded like a shallow excuse, though it was nothing but the truth. "Some trouble with the Haworth Home," he added, hoping to make it clear that he hadn't been frittering his time away at summer house parties, fishing expeditions, or whatever other nonsense occupied most young men of leisure during the summer months.

"Aye, stands to reason that an orphanage would keep you busy," Mr. Weston agreed. "You've been about the Lord's work, and your father ought to respect that!"

Walter grinned ruefully. "I doubt he'll see it that way." He'd known the Westons for years, and he saw no need to present a false front to them. Given the way country gossip traveled, they'd know the truth of the matter anyway, no matter what he might say.

His prediction proved entirely too accurate. When he arrived at the manor, he found his father out in the stable yard, watching the stable master doing groundwork with a handsome gray. Walter had never shared his father's interest in horses, but he'd sat through enough lectures on horse breeding and training to recognize that the colt had good conformation as well as an attractive coat pattern.

"He looks promising," Walter said, knowing that would please his father. "Is this one of Phantom's get?"

"Mm-hmm," Edward Haworth responded. "One of Portia's last foals. He'll make one half of a good carriage pair if I can find a match."

"Indeed." Matched grays were prized for carriages, especially by sporting young gentlemen who wanted to drive flashy equipages. Walter wracked his brains to think of something else he could say about the horse, but he could come up with nothing better than "What d'you call him, then?"

"Spectre, though everyone just says Specks." His father turned away from the horse to face Walter, and the corners of his mouth automatically tipped down. "You didn't come here to talk horses with me, did you?"

Walter sighed. The familiar scowl on his father's face made him seem like a delinquent school-boy rather than a grown man of seven-and-twenty. Even worse was the knowledge that his father viewed Walter as no more of an adult than he had ten years ago.

"No, sir," he agreed. "I came down from Lancashire because you asked me to."

"I've been asking you to come home for months," his father grumbled. "Your mother misses you, y'know."

"I know." Walter knew better than to expect his father to

admit to missing him, too. Even if it were true, which he could not be certain of. He drew a deep breath before he said something he knew his father wouldn't like. "I don't think I can stay long this time, Father. I'm still helping Ernest with a problem at the home."

"Ernest is perfectly capable of looking after an orphanage without your help," his father mendaciously declared. "It's what he's paid to do. You, on the other hand, ought to be learning how to manage the estate. Your grandfather bought this place for you. He wanted to give you a better position in society than he ever had. The least you could do is be grateful!" Though it was an old complaint, Haworth's tone hadn't lost any of his customary acrimony. If anything, he'd grown more bitter over the last few years.

"I know, Father." Walter wanted to argue, as he had done in the past, but by now he knew how futile that would be.

Neither his father nor his grandfather had ever understood that gentility did not hold the same value for Walter that it did for them. Perhaps, he suspected, this was because he'd been raised in an already-wealthy family, rather than having to work his way up. His grandfather, Frederic Haworth, had plotted, wheedled, and worked his way into being one of the wealthiest sugar merchants in the kingdom. By the time he'd amassed what he considered an adequate fortune, he'd been ready to retire and enjoy life.

Walter, on the other hand, had been born with all his grandfather's intelligence and energy, earning acclamations as a scholar both in public school and at Cambridge. But after he'd finished his training as a solicitor, he'd been allowed no adequate outlet for his abilities and interests.

The senior Haworth men assumed that Walter would devote his time and talent to playing the part of country gentleman—a position purchased for him at great cost. If Walter had been at all interested in livestock, apple orchards, or other agriculture, he might have been perfectly happy living at Northcote Manor and participating in local society. Unfortunately, his interests lay elsewhere, in medicine and the natural sciences. As a result, he was as much a disappointment in adulthood as he'd been a satisfaction in his youth. And his father never let him forget it.

"Have you greeted your mother yet?" Edward asked.

"No, sir. I stopped here first." Only then did Walter wonder why he'd gone straight to the farm rather than calling on his mother first. The decision probably said volumes about his childish desire to please his father.

"Let's go up to the house now, then," his father suggested. "I imagine you'd be glad of a cup of tea."

"I would indeed." However, he was even more interested in Mrs. Bantry's baking. She made the most divine fairy cakes, the like of which he'd never found anywhere else. Since Mrs. Bantry refused to share her recipe, he only got to enjoy his favorite treat when he came home.

When he reached the house, Walter ran up to his bedchamber, taking the stairs two at a time. His luggage had already been placed in his room, and someone had already fetched an ewer of hot water for him. Walter washed his hands and tidied up before he went down to the drawing room.

It was just as well that he did so, because he found his mother entertaining callers this afternoon. There were four ladies in the drawing room rather than the two he'd expected.

"Walter!" His mother's whole face lit up like a Vauxhall pyrotechnic display. She rose to her feet and hurried to embrace him.

"Hello Mother. Genie." He smiled and nodded at the two unfamiliar ladies. Given the facial similarities and the age gap between the two, he guessed them to be mother and daughter, though he'd never seen either of them before.

His mother soon remembered her good manners. She turned to the visitors with a smile and said "Mrs. Mitchell, Miss Mitchell, may I present to you my son, Walter? He's been away assisting with some of the charities my father-in-law founded." Whatever his father might think of Walter, his mother's voice radiated pride. "Walter, Mrs. Mitchell is the wife of the new rector, and this is her eldest daughter."

"Very pleased to meet you," Walter said, though he would, in fact, rather have had tea with just the family. Especially since Mrs. Mitchell's brilliant, toothy smile filled him with foreboding. Miss Mitchell looked so young he could not be certain she was already out, but the speculative looks her mother directed at him suggested that, despite her apparent youth, Miss Mitchell might already be on the hunt for a husband.

Tea passed as painfully as he expected. Miss Mitchell played the part of a bashful young debutante to perfection. She spoke in a soft voice, as if afraid to be overheard. She averted her eyes when her mother praised her singing voice. And when she took her leave, she lowered her head so she could shyly look up at Walter from under her eyelashes.

Perhaps Walter wronged her. Maybe none of that was an act, and Miss Mitchell really was bashful. He could not have said why he felt so cynical about her behavior. But he knew he hadn't imagined the Mitchells' interest in him, because the first thing his mother said after her callers left was, "And what did you think of Miss Mitchell, Walter?"

Walter restrained his desire to sigh or roll his eyes. His mother did not deserve such disrespect. "She seemed like a well-bred young lady." He hoped such temperate praise would discourage any further matchmaking on his mother's part. If not, reminding her of Miss Mitchell's youth might do the trick. "I suppose the child is not out of the schoolroom yet?"

"Don't be silly," his father groused. "She's a grown woman. Most popular girl in the county, I'd wager. At the last assembly in Stornley, she had all the young men lining up to dance with her."

"Good for her." This time, Walter couldn't keep the edge out of his voice.

His mother's smile fell. "She really is a pleasant girl, Walter. But of course, if there is anyone you like better, you need not concern yourself with Miss Mitchell."

He gritted his teeth. What on earth could he say to convince his mother to stop matchmaking? Unless... he sucked in his breath, shocked by the audacity of the idea that struck him. He darted a glance to his father, wondering if he could make this scheme work.

"As a matter of fact," he said diffidently, "there *was* a young lady in Ingleton who caught my eye."

Both his mother and his sister sprang to attention like a pair of pointers who'd found a covey of partridges. "Is that so?" his mother asked. "Tell us about her, Walter. Do we know her family?"

Walter bit his lip to keep from chuckling. "I don't believe you've met her parents," he said judiciously. "They do not move in the same circles we do."

"I hope you haven't gone and fallen in love with an entirely unsuitable girl," his father warned. "A grand house like this needs a fine lady at the helm. Someone who knows how to handle the reins of a country estate." Walter's father spoke with as much pride as if the Haworths had lived at Northcote for generations, rather than a mere decade.

"Mixing your metaphors, father?" Walter teased. But Edward Haworth's glare drove away Walter's amusement. "As it happens, I'm afraid *I* am the one who is unsuitable. I doubt her parents will consider me good enough for her."

If anything, his father grew even angrier. "I'd like to know who in the world would think *you* weren't good enough for their daughter! You're a fine figure of a gentleman, with a tidy estate waiting for you, and—"

Walter decided to cut this rant short before his father grew too worked up. "She is Lady Hester Bracknell, the daughter of the Marquis of Reading. I'm sure you can see why it is a hopeless fancy on my part. Her parents probably expect her to marry a nobleman."

A silence fell over the room. His mother stared at him with wide eyes. His father frowned.

Eugenia, on the other hand, looked amused. "Goodness,

Walt. When you decide to grab something out of life, you certainly aim for the highest prize, don't you?"

Walter chuckled. She had him there! "I suppose so." Then he turned a more serious face towards his mother. He didn't want to mislead her about the situation. "But really, it is only a fancy. I don't expect anything to come of it."

His mother looked as if she did not know what to say. Rather to Walter's surprise, it was his father who broke the silence this time. "If you ask me, even a duke's daughter ought to consider herself lucky to marry our boy."

"Exactly right!" Walter's mother chimed in. "You would make a good husband even for the finest of fine ladies."

Walter smiled. "I think you see me through rose-colored glasses," he said affectionately. "But enough of this nonsense. Why don't you tell me what's been happening in Stornley these days?"

Now that he'd managed to turn the conversation away from Miss Mitchell, he had rather not discuss Lady Hester any further. He knew very well it was a hopeless fantasy, but he did not care to belabor that point. Sometimes a man needed to take a moment to admire a brilliant star, no matter how far out of reach it twinkled.

Chapter Seventeen

July 1818

FRANK FINALLY RETURNED, melancholy from having ministered the final communion service to his dying friend. On the last day of June, Neville Butler departed Ingleton, hopefully forever. Hester said a few silent prayers of gratitude once he was gone. All this time, she'd been waiting for his next move. His leaving without having done anything after all was a pleasant surprise. Perhaps she'd overestimated the depths of his malice.

Rose was in much better spirits now that she had her husband back, though her baby still refused to make his or her appearance. "Maybe," she suggested one morning, "the baby is delaying so I have enough time to knit more stockings for it."

Hester giggled. "Don't you already have twenty pairs of stockings ready? How many feet do you expect this child to have?"

"You never know," Rose said darkly. "What if it's twins?"

The two women exchanged uneasy glances. Because they were so small, twin babies often did not survive. Hester silently hoped that her sister-in-law carried only one baby.

Before either of them could break the silence, one of the housemaids stepped into the room. "Lady Hester, there's a letter for you." She held out a thick packet appearing to contain more than the usual single page of correspondence.

"Oh?" Hester hadn't expected a letter, given how recently she'd replied to her mother's last message. "I hope it's not bad news."

Her father, Lord Reading, suffered from a condition that caused terrible pains in his legs and made all his movements clumsy. He had difficulty walking, even with a cane. None of the physicians' recommendations had brought him any relief, and everyone lived in fear of his condition worsening.

But when she saw the address on the envelope, she realized that it had been written by her father, not her mother. How odd! She couldn't remember the last time she'd gotten a letter directly from her father. Normally, her mother passed on any messages he might have for Hester.

Hester drew a deep breath and broke the familiar Bracknell family seal. The letter was long: her father had indeed used two pages. By the time she finished reading, she'd gone cold and numb from head to toe.

My Daughter,

When your mother sent you to Lancashire to visit your brother, it was with the understanding that you would behave with utmost propriety so as to avoid further discrediting the family name. Your mother and I believed that some time away from the temptations and pitfalls of London would be to your advantage. Though I had rather have called you home to Shropshire, your mother thought you could be of use to your sister-in-law.

I now regret that I agreed with her. You may imagine my dismay when I received word that you had been once again caught in a compromising situation, this time with the son of a sugar-merchant! I cannot imagine what madness compelled you to risk your reputation again, so soon after the last incident.

If you mean to seriously encourage the advances of a con-ceited young mushroom, I urge you to reconsider. Though marriages between people in trade and in fashionable society have sometimes been successful, you must consider that when a gentleman marries a woman of lower station, he elevates her to his station, whereas when a lady marries a man beneath her, the marriage degrades her rather than elevating her partner. Young Mr. Haworth is not even the son of a gentleman, let alone a nobleman. A marriage to him would remove you from your current elevated position and reduce you to the company of tradesmen and their families. Is that the life you want? I urge you to think very hard on the matter. You can have no conception of how your life would change if you marry Mr. Haworth.

In any case, the current state of affairs cannot be allowed to continue. If you intend to accept a proposal from Mr. Haworth, I must request that he call upon me at Bracknell Hall at his earliest convenience to discuss the terms of the marriage contract.

If, on the other hand, you meant only to flirt with a suitor whom you did not intend to accept, I must inform you that those tricks won't answer. You cannot afford another scandal, Hester. Unless you are about to repair your reputation through matrimony, I must insist that you return home.

Kindly reply by the earliest post to inform me of whether I may expect a call from Mr. Haworth, or if I am to send a carriage to Ingleton to collect you. At this point, your own folly has eliminated any other option.

Despite my disappointment I remain your loving father,
Reading

Hester stared blankly at the notepaper, frantically trying to figure out what series of mistakes could have resulted in this response. She hadn't flirted with anyone the entire time she'd been in Ingleton! Nor had Mr. Haworth given even the slightest sign of romantic interest in her. He'd certainly never attempted anything resembling a flirtation with her. On the contrary, he'd always behaved with the utmost propriety.

Now, if the letter had mentioned *Mr. Butler*, she would have understood what her father meant. Neville Butler had certainly tried to win her hand in marriage by hook or by crook. Someone might very well have reported the birthday party incident to her father. But what could possibly have led her father to think she had encouraged a suit from Mr. Haworth?

She was shaken out of her musings by a gentle hand on her shoulder. "Hester? Hester? Is something wrong? Is it bad news from home? Is someone unwell?" Rose peered down at her, concern written in every line of her face.

"Not exactly." Hester put the letter down on the nearest table and rubbed her hands together, trying to rid herself of that cold, clammy sensation. "That is, it's not *good* news, but no one is ill. It . . . it must be some sort of misunderstanding." She swallowed a lump in her throat and blinked her eyes rapidly, realizing she was on the verge of tears. "I need to talk to Frank."

"He has a meeting—"

"I know," she interrupted, not caring how rude she was being. "But it is rather an emergency. Please, can you go get Frank?" Her brother would know what to do. He *must* know what to do!

THAT EVENING, HESTER stood by the parlor window, looking out anxiously into the late summer twilight. Frank, after hearing her story, had insisted that they needed to speak to Walter Haworth, to see if he knew what this was about. Mr. Haworth had only that day returned from Bristol, but he agreed to drop in after dinner.

Hester had not been able to eat more than a few bites at dinner. Not surprisingly, the stress of receiving her father's letter had triggered one of her bad headaches, and the accompanying nausea meant she could not stomach a hearty meal.

Really, Hester ought to be lying in bed with a cold compress on her head. Better yet, she ought to be home in her own room at Bracknell Hall, resting while her sister or mother read aloud to her. She could not follow the plot of a novel when her headaches were at their worst, but sometimes the regular rhythm of metered poetry comforted her. Her mother liked to joke that she felt like young David, soothing the evil spirit out of King Saul with his music.

Well, it seemed she'd be going home soon enough. Once again, she'd be running home in disgrace; this time, for something she hadn't even done. She had willingly kissed Simon at that ill-fated ball, but she had done nothing to incur censure now. The unfairness of it brought tears to the corners of her eyes. She blinked them away, knowing that crying would only make her headache worse.

Voices in the front hall warned her that Frank had returned. She had just enough time to dash the tears away from her eyes before greeting her brother and Mr. Haworth.

Rather than take a seat, Mr. Haworth walked right up to Hester and took hold of her hand. He did not beat about the bush, but got straight to the point. "Lady Hester, I am so sorry if anything I have said or done has inadvertently led your family to erroneous conclusions. But I assure you that *I* did not spread whatever rumors your father may have heard." A flush rose on his cheekbones. "I would never spread malicious gossip about someone."

Hester squeezed his hand, as if he were the one in need of comfort. "I know you would never do such a thing, Mr. Haworth. But I cannot understand how my father could have gotten so confused. If he had accused me of flirting with Mr. Butler, now, the mistake would have been more understandable. . ."

Mr. Haworth sighed. He took his hand away so that he could remove his spectacles and examine the lenses, though they'd looked perfectly clean to her.

"As to that, I have a theory." He glanced at Frank and hesitated.

"A theory that seems plausible to me." Frank sounded angry. "Go ahead and tell her."

Mr. Haworth turned back to Hester. "I believe Butler himself may have originated this rumor in retaliation. The last time I spoke to him, he tried to get me to promise not to tell anyone about his trickery the night of the party. I refused to make any such promise." He scowled briefly. "And then he made some strange comments that seemed to suggest he thought *I* was courting you. Which was not the case." He flushed bright red. "Given that conversation, I suspect Butler was the source of whatever rumor or innuendo upset your parents so much."

"I see. I suppose your theory makes sense." She could readily imagine Butler stirring up trouble this way. It seemed consistent with his character, though she could not see how it would benefit him.

"He is even more of a scoundrel than we thought," Frank growled. "If I weren't a clergyman. . ." He let his voice trail off, apparently having thought better of whatever he meant to say.

Hester probably ought to be as angry as Frank, given that her reputation was at stake. Instead, she still felt numb. The only sensation that intruded on her awareness was the throbbing pain in her head. She put a hand to her forehead, wishing she could brush away the pain.

"You seem unwell, my lady." Mr. Haworth sounded less confident now. "Perhaps we should finish this discussion tomorrow?"

That prospect tempted Hester. She would very much like to lie down and rest. But she also wanted to get this conversation over with. "Is there much more to say? I still have many questions, but I suppose I won't get any answers until I speak to my father."

Mr. Haworth cleared his voice. "Of course, if you think it best to go home. . ."

Hester's eyes widened. "What other option do I have?" The words of her father's letter echoed in her mind: *"your own folly has eliminated any other options."* He was right about the lack of options, but wrong about the cause. "Neville Butler has taken away all my options. He has ruined me."

"Frank," Mr. Haworth said, "do you suppose I could have a moment to talk to your sister alone?"

"Oh?" Frank looked puzzled for a moment, then shrugged. "Of course." He turned to Hester and rested a comforting hand on her shoulder. "I'll see if someone can brew a cup of your peppermint and willow tea for you. That's what you take for your bad headaches, isn't it?"

"Yes, thank you." She forced a smile, though her face felt stiff from pain. After the door shut behind Frank, she glanced uncertainly at Mr. Haworth. What on earth could he possibly have to say to her that he didn't want her brother to hear? And why was Frank letting him speak to her without a chaperone when there were already rumors circulating about them? A meeting alone with Mr. Haworth would only make matters worse!

Mr. Haworth clasped his hands behind his back, looking unexpectedly nervous. "Lady Hester, I think perhaps we should sit down for this conversation. It may take some time."

A wave of foreboding crept over Hester. Her hands still felt frozen into lifelessness, but her heart began to pound heavily. Somehow, she knew what he would say, though she hadn't previously anticipated this development.

"Yes," she said breathlessly. "I think I had better sit down."

❧

Chapter Eighteen

WALTER WAITED FOR Lady Hester to sit down before taking his own seat. He chose a chair near enough that they could easily converse, but far enough that she would not feel threatened by his proximity. He nervously rubbed his hands along the sides of his trousers, wondering how to begin.

Some part of him was already convinced that speaking now was a colossal mistake. Lady Hester seemed to be in pain or shock. This could not be the right time to broach such an important subject.

On the other hand, she was right that Butler had taken away most of her options. If the former curate continued to spread false rumors about her behavior, he might very well permanently damage her reputation. If Walter could offer her an alternative to that—well, he had a duty to speak, didn't he?

Lady Hester cleared her throat and rested her clasped hands on her knees. "Mr. Haworth, if you are about to offer marriage to me in an attempt to salvage my reputation, let me assure you that although I appreciate the gesture, such a sacrifice is not necessary."

He raised his eyebrows. "Sacrifice?" She thought marrying her would be a *sacrifice*? "If anyone were to make a sacrifice," he pointed out, "it would be you. You would have to give up your life in the fashionable world. I can offer you nothing more than a gentleman's manor house and a quiet life in the country."

Her mouth fell ajar. She snapped it closed and drew her brows down, looking confused. "What manor house? I thought... aren't you a solicitor?" She did not add the word "only" before "solicitor," but it nevertheless echoed in Walter's mind.

He looked down at the floor, wishing he had not already given his spectacles an unnecessary cleaning a few minutes ago. His hands could have benefited from something to fidget with.

"I did train as a solicitor, yes. But I don't practice law. I only use my knowledge to help out the family, and to assist some of my grandfather's charities." He sighed, thinking of his last visit home, of his father's wish that Walter would return to Northcote Manor permanently. "Before my grandfather died, he purchased an estate in Somerset, not far from Bristol. He bequeathed it to my father. I am my father's only son, so. . ."

"Ah, I see. You are the heir to a landed estate. You are a gentleman." She blinked and shook her head. "My apologies, Mr. Haworth. I already knew that you were a gentleman in education, manners, and morals. I simply did not realize that you were a gentleman in the, ah, economic sense, too."

"I understand," he said quickly, not wanting to embarrass her. God knew this conversation was embarrassing enough already! "My father worked for many years as a merchant in the company my grandfather founded. But the company has since been sold to a couple of my distant cousins." Though Haworth & Haworth was still run by the family, Walter's branch had had nothing to do with it since his grandfather's death.

She nodded but kept staring at him with wide eyes and nervous posture. He wished he had any inkling of what she was thinking. For all he knew, she might be hoping he would conclude the conversation and leave her in peace.

He twisted his mouth into something that hopefully resembled a smile. "It was my grandfather's wish that his descendants live as members of the gentry." For reasons Walter did not fully understand, merely being wealthy had not satisfied Frederic Haworth. He wanted a high status to match his fortune. "Unfortunately, I am not particularly interested in agriculture. Even so, my father would like me to come home and help him run the estate, and of course the house is large enough for me to live there with a wife and—"

Oh, dear God, he was babbling inanely. The line between Lady Hester's brows had deepened, and her mouth hung ajar. He was probably only confusing her further. "I only mean to say, my lady, that if you married me, you would live the life of a country gentlewoman." That would mean setting aside his half-formed plan to apply for the position of manager of Sir Henry's children's hospital, but that had only been another of his castles-in-the-air, anyway.

If anything, the thoughtful lines in her face grew stronger. "I see. Thank you for more clearly representing your station in life. But I still think it would be best not to allow Mr. Butler to force either of us into an unwanted marriage. I had better return to Bracknell Hall."

Unwanted marriage. Walter's shoulders slumped. So that was it, then. There was no point in making an official proposal. He stared down at the floor, taking a moment to collect himself. He had not really expected any other answer, had he? Lady Hester would probably marry another aristocrat. If not a nobleman, then a nobleman's son. Still, perhaps he could help her yet.

"As to that, I have an alternative suggestion," he said diffidently. "If you will allow me, I will travel to Bracknell Hall on your behalf. It is in Shropshire, I think Frank said? Only two days away?" When she nodded, he continued speaking. "I think I can better explain the real situation in person rather than in writing. I hope to persuade your father to relent."

"It is very kind of you to offer, Mr. Haworth," Lady Hester said. "But there is no need for you to go to such trouble on my account."

"It is no trouble at all," he insisted. "Especially since I have a few other matters I wish to discuss with Lord Reading."

He did not look forward to meeting Lord Reading face-to-face, but at least that way, he would be able to answer the marquis's questions. And it would be easier for Walter to tell what the marquis really thought of him as a potential suitor.

Not that there was any point in further pursuing Lady Hester, he reminded himself. She remained what he had once thought her: a brilliant but distant star, twinkling like a jewel placed far beyond his reach. A man might admire such a luminary, but he could not pluck it from the heavens and take it home with him, could he? And now he was getting fanciful! Walter shook his head, trying to clear his mind.

Lady Hester frowned. "Is something wrong, Mr. Haworth?"

"No, no." He cleared his throat. "I also wanted to ask if I could borrow the letter about your brother." She looked puzzled, so he quickly clarified. "I mean the one that mentions someone named L. blackmailing Lord Crowthorne."

Walter hadn't been able to stop thinking about that letter. It ought to have been none of his business, but having found the letter, he felt responsible for the discovery. Perhaps he'd been smitten with detective fever, but Walter wanted to ask the marquis some questions. Lord Reading might know more about the blackmail than Lady Hester did.

"Oh, I suppose that would be all right," she said doubtfully. "My brother Frank has the letter at the moment, though. Would you like me to get it from him?"

"Ah, no, I will ask him myself." He ought to discuss his plans with Frank, anyway. Lady Hester's brother might have questions of his own for Walter to ask Lord Reading.

"Very well. Thank you for being willing to speak to my father."

They both rose to their feet. Lady Hester moved as gracefully as ever, but Walter felt like an overgrown giraffe. Not for the first time, he wished he'd been built on more graceful lines, and of a more moderate height. He had no need to be this tall! Towering over other people was not always the advantage shorter men seemed to assume.

"I must wish you a good journey." This time, Lady Hester did not offer him her hand in farewell. On the contrary, she kept her hands tightly clasped together.

"Thank you. And, er, thank you for hearing me out, despite the unfortunate circumstances that brought me here tonight." Walter very nearly cringed at the sound of his own voice. Did he always sound this prosy?

Lord, but he would have made a sorry excuse for a suitor! Lady Hester ought to be wooed with all the poetry and romance her heart desired. In the long run, though, there could be no benefit to pretending to be something he was not. Walter was not, in fact, romantic, poetic, or sentimental. If Lady Hester required those traits in a suitor, she probably wouldn't have liked having Walter as a husband. It was just as well that he realized that now, before he made a fool of himself.

"Of course, you are always most welcome here," Lady Hester said. "Was there anything else you wanted, Mr. Haworth?"

"No, no. I shall be on my now." He sketched a clumsy bow, then left the room with graceless haste. He wished he could simply go home without speaking to anyone else, but he really did need to speak to Frank.

Frank was in his study, writing something that Walter suspected was a sermon. He put down his pen and smiled. "How did it go, then? Any luck?"

Walter shook his head. "I did not propose to her after all. Not formally, anyway. She made it clear that she did not want to marry just to save her reputation." His throat tightened up alarmingly, but he tried to ignore it. "And she is right. I do not want to marry an unwilling bride. In the long run, that could not be conducive to anyone's happiness."

"Are you sure, old chap? I rather thought her opinion of you had improved lately. I mean—" Frank came to a stumbling halt and flushed bright red as he realized what he'd implied.

"It doesn't matter," Walter quickly said. "It was a foolish pipe dream, anyway. But enough of that!" He forced his mouth into a stiff smile and changed the subject. "I was wondering if I could take that letter I found in Butler's room with me? The one about blackmail? I suspect your father would be very interested in it."

"You're probably right about that." Frank pulled open a drawer in his desk and rummaged about for a moment before he found the letter. "I do wish I knew who this L. person is," he grumbled. "I'd like to have a word with him!"

"So would I!" Walter replied. Whatever Lord Crowthorne's sins, he surely didn't deserve to be blackmailed.

Frank handed the letter to Walter, then peered up at him, frowning. "You really don't have to go dashing off to Shropshire on our behalf, you know. I could go in your stead."

Walter raised his eyebrows. "You would leave Rose when she's so near her confinement?" Technically, she had passed her estimated date of confinement, although the monthly nurse kept reminding everyone about the "estimated" part.

Frank sighed. "Well, no, I suppose not. She'd be extremely unhappy about that. As would I." The corner of his mouth tugged up. "I do worry about her a good deal, you know."

"I know," Walter said gently. "She is in good hands with you." Both of his cousins had married well, and not only in the sense of marrying into elevated families. Both Ivy and Rose had found husbands who loved them deeply.

Maybe someday Walter would find such matrimonial comfort, too. But not now. Lady Hester had made that very clear. He ought to put her out of his head entirely. At least, he ought to do so once he'd gotten over this interview with Lord Reading. For Lady Hester's sake, he hoped he could persuade her father that it was not necessary for them to marry. There must be some better way to silence the rumor mill and defeat Neville Butler's machinations.

Chapter Nineteen

NEARLY A WEEK after she received the fateful letter from her father, Hester awoke with another one of her pulsing headaches. This time, her megrim had probably been provoked by a change of weather. When she peered out the window, Hester saw dark clouds overhead—the sort that might carry thunder, lightning, and high winds as well as rain. For some reason, stormy weather nearly always gave her a headache. She was probably in for a rough day.

All morning long, the storm clouds glowered overheard, withholding the threatened rain. At luncheon, both Hester and Rose toyed with their cold meat and salad.

"Are you unwell, too?" Hester asked her sister-in-law. So far as she knew, Rose did not get headaches like hers.

Rose pulled a face. "Everything hurts this morning. I think I may have some digestive upset."

Frank's face paled. "That's all we need in the village. A bad case of dysentery." He shuddered. "Is that what you have too, Hester?"

Hester shook her head but immediately regretted it, because the motion hurt. "This is just one of my usual sick headaches. I think it's the fault of the weather. There must be a storm coming in."

"Well, let me know if either of you need me to call on the

apothecary," Frank offered. "I'm happy to ride into Rocheford if necessary."

But he did not have the opportunity to do so. Before he'd even finished his luncheon, a young boy came to the door with the message that a farmer working on a fence had suffered some sort of apoplexy. They'd sent for the surgeon, but when Mr. Wright woke up, he'd asked for a clergyman, too.

The problem was that Mr. Wright lived on a remote free-holding across the river, at least an hour's ride away. Frank wavered for a moment, clearly torn about whether or not he should leave his wife and sister alone in their current ill-health.

"You had better go," Rose advised him. "There's no clergy-man nearer to hand, is there? And you haven't a curate you can send in your place. You need not worry about me, love. I'll put my feet up and rest, like I'm supposed to, and I'll be fine. I have Mrs. Potter to look after me now, remember?" Mrs. Potter was the monthly nurse.

"As for me, I only need a cup of my headache tea and a dark, quiet room to rest in," Hester reminded Frank. "Go see this Mr. Wright. He probably needs your help more than we do."

True to her word, Hester drank a cup of her medicinal tea. Then she went upstairs to lie down in her room with the curtains drawn, a cold compress on her forehead, and the door locked against any intrusion. Despite the throbbing pain, she easily fell into a natural, peaceful slumber, devoid of nightmares.

That afternoon, the storm broke. A howling gust of wind rattled the shutters and startled Hester out of her sleep. She sat up, so confused that at first, she didn't even notice that her headache had receded. All that remained was the dull, tender, "bruised" feeling she sometimes experienced at the end of one of her attacks. If she was lucky, the headache would be gone entirely in another day.

Unfortunately, Rose's condition had not improved. Hester found her pacing back and forth in the parlor, a grimace on her face.

"Is it a digestive ailment after all?" Hester suggested. She certainly hoped Frank was wrong about dysentery!

Rose shook her head. "It's contractions." She stopped walking and put a hand to her side. "Coming every five minutes and getting stronger."

Hester clapped a hand over her mouth. "You're in labor?" she squealed.

Rose gritted her teeth against the pain but nodded. Then she sighed as the contraction eased. "I'm not certain but. . . I think so. I think this might be it." Her face displayed equal parts fear and exhilaration.

"Have you sent for your medical attendant yet?" Hester ran her mind over all the things that needed to be done. "What about Frank? Is he still away?"

"Yes, I sent for the surgeon who delivers babies around here, and no, Frank isn't back yet. The rain may keep him away for a while." She rested her hands on her rounded belly and stared out the window.

"Oh!" Hester hadn't thought about the weather interfering with travel. She peered out the window. The rain fell lightly but steadily, a shower rather than a downpour, thank goodness. "It's not too bad yet. Maybe he'll still make it home in time."

"I hope so, because the Old Bridge sometimes gets underwater in heavy rains. The bridge really needs to be rebuilt, but it's technically outside our parish, and no one seems to listen to complaints—ah!" Another contraction must have struck Rose, because she snapped her mouth shut, grimacing at the pain.

"Is there anything you can do for the pain?" Hester wondered. She could not help imagining how she would feel if she were in Rose's position. Of course, if she married, she might very well face the pains of labor someday. She wasn't at all sure how she felt about that prospect.

Rose waited to speak until the contraction ended. "Mrs. Potter recommends walking during labor as long as I can. She said I should try to relax between contractions. As if anyone could relax when they know there's more pain coming!"

Why didn't people take laudanum during labor? Hester wondered. She did not care for all the effects of the drug, but in Rose's current state, relief from pain might be worth a clouded mind or strange nightmares. But this didn't seem like the right time to ask such questions. There were more practical concerns at hand.

"Can I get you anything to eat or drink?" She had no idea whether women in labor were supposed to eat, but standing aside and watching Rose suffer made her feel worse than useless.

"A cup of tea, maybe?" Rose suggested. "Oh, and could you fetch a blanket from the linen closet? I keep shivering, too."

For the next half-hour, Hester alternated between helping Mrs. Potter prepare the delivery room and running errands for Rose. There was no room in the vicarage for a separate birthing chamber, so Rose would deliver in her own bedchamber. Mrs. Potter changed the linens on the bed and put a separate set of clean sheets on the dressing table, so that the bed linens could be changed again as soon as the birth was over. Hester helped the nurse take down the hanging bed curtains to allow the air in the room to circulate.

"Normally, we'd open up the window," Mrs. Potter explained, "But we'll have to wait until the rain lets up to do that."

Glancing out the window at the steadily driving rain, Hester had to agree.

Lady Inglewhite arrived not long after that. While she comforted Rose, Hester played the part of an ineffectual bystander. This must be why men often weren't allowed to attend childbirths, she decided. They wouldn't like having to admit that there was nothing they could do to help!

Then they waited. Hester had naively assumed that the beginning of true labor meant the baby would arrive today. Lady Inglewhite and Mrs. Potter enlightened her on that point. Her eyes grew wider as she listened to the two women exchange stories of long, difficult labors they had attended or heard about. They had the wisdom or courtesy to refrain from sharing such anecdotes within Rose's hearing, but Hester heard enough to horrify her.

As day turned into night, the gentle rainfall turned into a downpour. The wind howled around the house and sent rain lashing against the windows. And still neither Frank nor the surgeon appeared. Where were they?

"Frank won't be able to travel in that weather." Rose sounded as if she were near tears. "By now the bridge will be underwater."

"He could go the long way around," Lady Inglewhite suggested. "The New Bridge never gets flooded. But it might be best for him to stay safely under a roof and wait out the storm. It can't last forever, Rose." She took Rose's hand, wincing when the laboring woman squeezed hard during the next contraction.

"Is there nothing I can do?" Hester wondered.

Under normal circumstances, she might have been sent out of the way. Unmarried girls did not often assist at childbirths. Traditionally, that was work for wives and widows. But she couldn't simply close her eyes and ignore Rose's travail.

"Why don't you read to me?" Rose said. "Something simple?"

"You might read the Psalter," Lady Inglewhite suggested.

Though Hester was not particularly devout, this seemed as good a suggestion as any. She fetched her Prayer Book and began with the first psalm.

In the next break between contractions, Rose turned to Hester. "Try reading the *De Profundis*." She must have seen the confusion on Hester's face, because she immediately clarified: Psalm 130.

Hester flipped through the gilt-edged pages of the prayer book until she found it. "Out of the depths I cry unto thee," she intoned. She had no idea whether her reading was at all helpful to Rose, but she herself drew a surprising comfort from the familiar rhythm of the psalm. "I look for the Lord; my soul doth wait for him . . ." Yes, she could see why Rose had thought of this passage.

She read onward, not particularly caring what she read so long as she could keep the even flow of words going. And still they waited. For the storm to end. For Frank to come home. For a successful conclusion to Rose's travails.

AT FOUR IN the morning on the tenth of July, Rose's baby finally made his grand entrance into the world. By then, the thunder had rolled away and the rain clouds had started breaking up, leaving only a few desultory showers. Little Alistair Bracknell took his first breath and promptly began screaming.

"Here, you take him, deary." Mrs. Potter handed the wet, slimy newborn to Hester.

Startled, Hester came very close to dropping her nephew, but Lady Inglewhite helped her clean him up and wrap him in soft, unbleached cotton.

Everything had gone very well. The surgeon, Mr. Newman, reached the vicarage before nightfall, despite the heavy rain. Not that he'd had all that much to do. Though he carried with him an *accoucheur's* bag of tools, he had never even needed to open it. For the most part, he sat back and gave Rose space to labor as she felt best. Everyone agreed that for a first birth, all had gone surprisingly well.

Except that Frank hadn't returned in time for the birth. Mr. Newman assured them that he'd probably been detained by the state of the Old Bridge. Crossing it had been difficult enough when the surgeon tried it; it would have gotten worse by the time Frank reached the river. Everyone agreed that was a perfectly plausible explanation. Even so, Rose bemoaned his absence until her attention was taken by more urgent matters.

Now, after all the cleaning and crying and struggles to nurse were over, both Rose and the baby slept soundly. Baby Alistair had been wrapped in swaddling bands and tucked into a rocking cradle. Later, he would be moved into the nursery, but for now he shared his mother's room.

Hester settled into a rocking chair in the corner of the room, having promised to keep an eye on the baby. But, having stayed up all night with everyone else, she soon drifted off to sleep. She dreamed about baby ducklings carrying umbrellas while they splashed in puddles. Why, she wondered, did they bother with the umbrellas if they were going to jump into a puddle anyway?

"Hetty," a familiar voice whispered, "is everyone well?"

"Hmm?" She blinked away visions of ducklings and looked around the room. The curtains had been drawn to allow mother and baby to sleep, but morning light filtered in around the edges. And there was Frank, finally. "Oh, you're back!"

"I am so sorry to have missed this." Frank stepped over to the bed, studied his sleeping wife for a moment, then leaned down to brush a kiss against her forehead.

Embarrassed, Hester averted her eyes. "I should probably go to bed and get a proper nap." Frank might want time alone with his wife and child.

He straightened up and turned towards Hester. "Before you go, there's something I need to tell you."

"Yes?" She smothered a yawn.

"I heard a rumor that Neville Butler is still in the area."

"What?" Hester stared at her brother. "But he left. Didn't he?" He'd been gone for days! She'd practically celebrated his exit.

Frank nodded. "That's what I thought, but apparently, he didn't go far. He's been seen just a few miles away. Someone told me he's staying at the Gray Goose Inn. It's probably nothing to worry about, but I thought you should know. . . just so it won't be a surprise if you run into him."

Or if he plays some new trick. Hester didn't voice her suspicion. The worry lines on Frank's face suggested that the possibility of further retaliation troubled him, too.

"Don't worry too much, Hetty." Frank stepped away from the cradle so he could rest a comforting hand on her shoulder. "You ought to go take that nap. You look done in."

"I am," she admitted. "Childbirth is hard work for everyone."

Rose had suffered the most, but they'd all experienced a year's worth of anxiety, hope, and joy in a single night.

Hester rose to her feet and took hold of Frank's hand, giving it an affectionate squeeze. "Congratulations on becoming a father, by the way." He was the first of her siblings to make the step into marriage and parenthood, so this felt like a new era for the whole Bracknell family.

She yawned again, then crept down the hall to her room. Never in her life had a soft pillow felt so well deserved.

Chapter Twenty

WALTER TRAVELED HARD and fast for two days, eager to report on both his meeting with Lord Reading and the letter he'd just received from Ernest Robinson. If he'd left even a few hours earlier, he'd have missed that letter, but the butler at Bracknell Hall handed it to him just before he stepped into the waiting carriage. He'd read it during the drive to the posting inn, and it gave him something new to think about apart from his regret over his abandoned courtship.

Ernest reported that, according to both Mr. Hunt, Neville Butler's handwriting was a match for the fraudulent ledger entries. They'd taken both the ledger and the note in Butler's writing to the local magistrate, Sir Hugo Chaloner, who agreed that the writing in the ledger looked suspiciously similar to the note in Butler's hand. Sir Hugo signed a warrant for Butler's arrest.

Walter read that letter over and over again, anticipation buzzing in his bones. This was exactly what they needed. All he had to do now was find Butler, and then he could be taken back to Somerset for questioning. Walter did not particularly care what happened to Butler once he was handed over to the magistrate. The case would be in the hands of the law then.

Lord Reading had offered to loan Walter a traveling chariot to take him back to Lancashire, but Walter had refused as politely as he could. A post chaise was perfectly adequate for his needs, and he did not wish to inconvenience the Reading family by borrowing their coachman for so long.

What he did not say was that he would've felt embarrassed, if not outright ashamed, to barrel down the road in a carriage marked with someone else's coat-of-arms, forcing lesser mortals to make way for him. That simply wasn't who Walter Haworth *was*.

Probably just as well, then, that he would not marry Lady Hester. As a son-in-law, Walter would have been a disappointment to the Bracknell family. Lord Reading had assured Walter that he would not stand in the way of his suit if he did try to woo Lady Hester, but they both knew that Walter would not have been anyone's first choice of suitor.

But Walter did his best not to brood over his disappointed heart. He had other, more important things to worry about. If he could do nothing else to help Lady Hester, he hoped to at least find out more about the scoundrel blackmailing her older brother. After his meeting with Lord Reading, he had a few clues to guide him.

Walter had hoped to reach the safety and comfort of Selwyn Castle that night. He would have had a good chance of doing so, if not for the blasted thunderstorm! Instead, the rain forced him off the road and into a rather dingy little inn. The dining room was overcrowded, the food was overcooked, and the innkeeper overcharged for both the meal and Walter's room.

Just as Walter contemplated abandoning the noise, smells, and grease of the taproom for the dubious comfort of his bedchamber, a gentleman dripping with rain stomped into the room, calling for a tankard of ale.

Surely, that couldn't be—? Walter twisted around in his chair for a better look. But it was. Neville Butler and a gray-haired stranger some years his senior had taken a booth not far from Walter's table. Butler must not have seen Walter, though, because he chatted with his companion, ignoring the other diners.

For one absurd moment, Walter toyed with the possibility of somehow disguising himself. If he took off his spectacles, and covered his distinctive yellow hair with a hat, would he escape notice? He doubted it. He was entirely too memorable and recognizable. Sometimes that was to his advantage, but tonight it felt like a distinct liability.

While he internally debated the best course of action, the question was taken out of his hands. Neville Butler happened to glance across the room. The moment he spied Walter, his eyes widened, and he slammed down his tankard of ale. Ale slopped out onto the table and onto his hand, but the usually tidy Mr. Butler ignored the mess as he stared at his archenemy.

At least, Walter thought of them as archenemies. Perhaps Butler thought of him as no more than a nuisance. But now might be the time to change that. Walter waved his hand to summon the serving girl.

"Yes, sir?" She had a smear of what looked like flour across one cheek, and several strands of curly hair had escaped from the bun at the back of her head. "Was there something you needed?"

He beckoned her to lean closer to him so he could whisper in her ear. "You had better tell the innkeeper that there's a wanted criminal in the room. We'll need a couple of strong men to detain him. He must not get away." Then, more loudly, he added, "And another pint of your best brew, if you please."

For a moment, she looked confused. But she must have been a quick study. She smiled, winked at him, and hurried over to the bar to pass the message on to the innkeeper.

Walter sat back down and forced himself to look away from Butler. He had no idea what his expression looked like at the moment, and he worried he'd give himself away if he caught Butler's eye again.

The wait for the innkeeper felt interminable, though it could only have been a matter of minutes. When the innkeeper reached Walter's table to ask what was wrong, Walter risked a quick glance at Butler.

That must have been enough warning for the former curate. He rose up from his seat, muttered something to his companion, and turned towards the door.

Time to skip the explanations. "He's getting away!" Walter yelled. He grabbed the innkeeper by the shoulder and turned him towards Butler, so he could see for himself the quick strides Butler took towards the exit.

Fortunately, the innkeeper did not demand any further explanations before springing into action. "Stop thief!" he bellowed.

Butler did not even pause to glance over his shoulder. He bolted for the door. But more than half the occupants of the pub bolted after him, raising the hue and cry. Butler might have been fast on his feet, but he didn't have a chance against the mob, especially when the innkeeper's wife barred the door, preventing his escape.

Walter, trailing at the back of the pack, could not see the moment when the mob grabbed Butler, but he heard the crowd's triumphant cry. He released his breath, adjusted his glasses, and went to explain the situation more fully to the innkeeper.

Most of the other members of the crowd returned to their seats in the taproom, eagerly discussing the arrest. As the crowd in the inn's entryway gradually thinned, Walter made his way to where two stout men restrained Butler.

"There you are, sir," the innkeeper addressed Walter. "D'you care to tell us what wrong this gentleman has done you?"

"He stole from orphans," Walter said bluntly.

The innkeeper's wife gasped and covered her face with her hands. The men restraining Butler scowled even more fiercely.

"That is to say," Walter clarified, "he embezzled money from an orphanage. He falsified ledgers by inflating the cost of provisions, then pocketed the change."

"That's a lie!" snapped Neville Butler. He lifted his chin and stared at Walter. "Can you prove this allegation?" His skeptical tone implied that the answer was "no."

The innkeeper frowned as he looked back and forth between Walter and Butler. "I dunno anything about embezzlement, sir. That's not the kind of theft we get around here. When you called 'stop thief,' I took it to mean that he'd stolen from *you*."

"Oh, but stealing from the poor orphans is worse, Martin," his wife said. "What kind of man takes food from the mouths of babes?"

"The orphanage in question was endowed by my grandfather, and I'm on the board that manages it," Walter explained. "So, the crime is, in a way, personal to me. But I can assure you that a magistrate has issued a warrant for Mr. Butler's arrest. At the very least, Mr. Butler must be brought back to Somerset for questioning. In capturing him, you've done nothing but your civic duty."

Butler's insouciance faded at the sound of the word "warrant." He gazed at each of the men detaining him, and his shoulders slumped.

"I am innocent," he insisted, "but if I am wanted for questioning, of course I must return to Somerset. I suppose *you* mean to bring me back, Mr. Haworth?" The sneering curl of his lip implied there was something ridiculous about that.

Walter hesitated for a moment. He hadn't thought this part through very well, had he? If he escorted Butler back to Somerset, he wouldn't be able to share the results of his meeting with Lord Reading with either Frank or Lady Hester. Besides, he was a solicitor, not a barrister. His legal training didn't include instructions on how to capture and convey a criminal.

"I'm not sure what the best procedure is," he admitted. "Perhaps he should be held at the nearest jail until we can consult a local magistrate?"

"The magistrate is Squire Anderson," the innkeeper's wife informed him. "But the rain'll keep him from leaving Greyfriar's Hall tonight." She peered up at her husband. "We'd best lock him an empty room for the night, Martin. No one'll want to take him to jail during this downpour."

Butler looked relieved by that suggestion, probably assuming that a room at an inn would be more comfortable and less humiliating than a jail cell. But as the innkeeper and his cronies led Butler away, the curate glanced over his shoulder, scowling so fiercely that Walter flinched. If looks could kill, Butler would be wanted for murder, too.

By morning, the rain had stopped. Much as Walter wanted to get on his way immediately, he thought it most wise to speak with Butler before he was moved to the nearest jail cell. Thefts of property worth more than a shilling were punished by hanging. Walter hoped Butler would be willing to talk in more detail in exchange for being charged with a lesser crime.

The two men met in Butler's room, with the local constable on hand as a guard. A spark of vindictive joy lit up Walter's face when he saw that for once, Butler did not look like a Bond Street Beau. Butler's cravat hung crookedly, his topcoat had been torn, and his usually flawless hair lay in disarray.

"Come to gloat over me, Mr. Haworth?" Dark anger burned in Butler's eyes. "That seems downright unchristian of you."

Walter ignored Butler's acrimony. "I wanted to ask you a few questions before you were removed to the care of a magistrate," he explained.

"I don't have a word to say to you." Butler jutted his chin out belligerently. "You can't prove that I stole anything. Anyone could have tampered with those ledgers!"

"Oh, I'm not going to ask about the embezzlement charges," Walter told him. A puzzled line formed between Butler's brows. Walter stalled any questions by clearing his throat, purely so he could enjoy that look of confusion a little longer. "I want to ask you about the blackmailer who has evidence about C. Who is L.? Where can he be found?"

Butler's mouth fell open. Clearly, he had not anticipated this question. He probably had no idea that Walter had ever snooped through his mail.

He gulped. "I don't see how that's any of your business, Mr.

Haworth. Nor is it my business, for that matter. Neither of us have anything to do with the Br—with the family in question, do we?"

Walter tightened his lips, irritated that Butler had come so close to identifying the Bracknell family by name. He had deliberately chosen to use only letters, since the two of them weren't alone in the room.

"As a friend of the family in question, I am concerned with anything that affects them. I know that the family deeply desires C. to return home." Especially since Lord Reading's health continues to decline. Crowthorne might become the sixth Marquis of Reading within the next few years, and his family hopes he'd return to England before then.

"Even if I knew who L. was, it might be dangerous to identify him," Butler pointed out. "A man willing to blackmail a member of the aristocracy wouldn't scruple to crush me. Am I expected to risk my life for a man I've never met?"

Walter sighed. He hadn't wanted to use any unfair influence, but what choice had he? He rose to his feet and pushed his chair back in place. Then he paused, as if struck by a sudden thought.

"Before I go," Walter said, "I ought to mention that the magistrate who signed the warrant is Sir Hugo Chaloner, who happens to have been a good friend of my grandfather's. I might be able to put in a good word for you, should you need it." He shrugged his shoulders, as if Butler's fate did not matter to him in the slightest.

Butler muttered something under his breath that might have been *bastard*. "I'm sure that if you wrack your brains, you might think of some members of the *ton* whose surnames start with L. There are many, after all. Lawrence, Lucas, Lowell. . ." He raised his eyebrows as he emphasized the final name.

"Is that so? I shall have to look into those names." Especially the name Lowell. "I will be certain to write to Sir Hugo about the embezzlement case." Walter deliberately refrained from describing the contents of that letter, letting Butler assume whatever he wanted to.

"*Sir Hugo.*" Butler scowled as he shook his head. "He won't remember me, but he was my mother's godfather."

Walter froze in place, though his heart beat more quickly. "Oh? I didn't realize you were from Somerset."

"I'm not, but my mother was a Maberly," Butler snapped. "She was born at Maberly Manor, long before your grandfather bought it." He scowled fiercely at Walter. "By rights, it ought to belong to us yet."

"Is that so? Well, in any case, I will make sure to remind Sir Hugo of the connection. Perhaps he still holds a soft spot for your family." Walter nodded to the constable as he left the room.

So much about the case made more sense in light of that information! The building that now housed the Haworth Home had belonged to the Maberly family decades ago, but it had been sold to cover the late Mr. Maberly's debts. That might explain why Butler had chosen to commit a crime with so little benefit to himself. If the crime was personal, more might have been at stake than shillings and pence.

Later, Walter would have letters to write to Ernest Robinson, Lord Rufford, and Sir Hugo. For now, though, he had a personal mission of his own. It was time to return to Ingleton and tell Lady Hester about his meeting with her father.

Chapter Twenty-One

AFTER STAYING UP all night, Hester had expected to sleep well into the afternoon. Heaven knew she needed rest! But Mrs. Potter shook her awake at noon.

"Miss! I mean, Lady Hester! There's a visitor who wishes to speak to you!"

Hester sat up and rubbed her eyes. "What now? Can you say that again?" She smothered a yawn.

She'd expected visitors who wanted to see Rose and the new baby. The vicar was an important member of the community in a village like this, and the birth of his first child would be a memorable event. But she hadn't expected any visitors who wanted to see *her*. Who on earth could be calling?

"It's a young gentleman," Mrs. Potter explained.

For one panicked moment, Hester worried that the putative "gentleman" might be Neville Butler himself. Why else would he linger in the area?

She was relieved when Mrs. Potter added: "A Mr. Haworth, I think he said?"

"Tell him I'll be down in—er, in about five minutes." She knew that was a generous estimate, given that she'd fallen asleep still wearing yesterday's soiled gown.

In reality, it took more like a quarter of an hour to wash up, dress, and tidy her hair. Her heart pounded with anticipation as she chose her prettiest morning gown. Utter silliness, she knew. She did not need to impress Mr. Haworth with her beauty or charm. But she wanted to look her best today, though she shied away from asking herself why that mattered so much.

She found the visitor in the parlor, in earnest discussion with Frank.

"Ah, Hetty, good to see you awake." Frank made a show of pulling out his watch, feigning amazement at the hour. "I'm afraid I've letters to write!"

Though Hester stared at him beseechingly, Frank only smiled at her as he left the room, once again leaving her alone with a handsome young man. The only comfort was that Mr. Haworth seemed to feel as tense and uncomfortable as Hester did. Her nerves might be wound tight, but at least she had company in her nervousness.

"I hear that your sister-in-law is to be congratulated on the birth of a son," he offered.

That drew a genuine smile from Hester and eased some of her awkwardness. "Yes. Little Alistair seems to be a fine, healthy child."

Rose thought Alistair was the most beautiful baby in the world, but Hester had her doubts. Even after being bathed, he seemed rather wrinkly and red to her. Mrs. Potter claimed all newborns looked like that, but Hester remained unconvinced.

After that, she fell silent, not knowing what to say. Mr. Haworth did not seem to know what to say, either. First, he took a small, leather-bound notebook out of his pocket. Then he made a show of examining the point of his pencil to see if it was sharp enough for writing.

She cautiously broached the awkward silence. "So. Did you meet with my father?" She clasped her hands together, feeling unexpectedly anxious. Her father's letter had sounded terribly angry. She could only hope that his bad temper had passed before Walter reached Bracknell Hall.

Mr. Haworth smiled. "Yes, I did meet with him. Once he

understood the situation, he received me most graciously."

The corner of his mouth quirked up, suggesting that perhaps Lord Reading hadn't behaved so pleasantly at first. Then Mr. Haworth looked down at the notebook in his hands, as if he needed to refresh his memory of the conversation.

"What did he say?" While she waited for his answer, Hester saw that each of her hands tightly clutched her skirt. That would not do! She smoothed out the skirt and folded her hands neatly in her lap, hoping to appear less anxious.

"After I explained things, he realized that the situation had been misrepresented to him, and he agreed that he'd overreacted." Mr. Haworth shot an odd, quick glance over the top of his lenses. "He's taken back the threat of summoning you back to Bracknell Hall. Though, of course, you are welcome to return home if you wish."

At that moment, a distant wail sounded from one of the rooms upstairs. The baby was awake and unhappy about something. The sound of galloping feet indicated that the either the nurse or one of the maids was rushing to assist, since Rose was not supposed to leave her bed.

"I think I might still be needed here," Hester suggested. "Babies seem to take a lot of work." Mrs. Potter rather alarmingly claimed the baby might grow even fussier and more demanding after the first couple of weeks. If that was true, Hester's help might be needed even more.

"Yes, I told Lord Reading that your sister-in-law might appreciate your assistance during her lying-in." He blinked owlishly. "However long that takes."

"Her doctor advises her to stay in bed for at least a couple of weeks," Hester explained. "Though I don't know if she will really do it. She was supposed to spend all her time resting before the baby arrived, and you could see for yourself how well that worked." Rose insisted that the resting regime made her feel worse.

"Yes, I'd be surprised if she decided to strictly follow the lying-in rules. In any case, your father wants me to tell you that you are welcome to stay here as long as you wish, or as long as your brother's family needs you."

Hester let out a tiny sigh of relief. "So, he's no longer trying to force us to marry, then?" she asked hopefully.

For some reason, the question put a flush on Mr. Haworth's face. "Um, no, he won't insist on it." He turned the pages in his notebook as if he were searching for a specific bit of information. "He did want you to know that he thought marrying might be the best way to protect your reputation from any further scandals."

Hester narrowed her eyes, suddenly guessing why Mr. Haworth seemed so bashful about this. "You mean he still wants me to marry you?"

His blush deepened. "That may be putting it too strongly. Let us say rather that he wishes you to consider it." He cleared his throat. "Believe me, I fully appreciate the awkwardness of this situation. I am aware that you don't want to marry me, and—"

She rushed to reassure him. "It's not that I want to NOT marry you, but rather that I don't *want* to marry you. If you see the difference."

Mr. Haworth gaped at her. "I'm. . . not sure that I do see the difference, but in any case, you may be assured that no one will force your hand on the matter."

"Good? I mean, good." A wave of doubt swept over her, leaving her momentarily uneasy about her decision. What would life have been like married to Walter Haworth? Would she have a better chance of having a marriage of mutual support and affection with him than with some young sprig of fashion she met in town?

Hester shook her head and tried to dismiss those doubts. It wasn't as if Mr. Haworth wanted to marry her. He had only offered in order to save her reputation. She didn't want to trap him in an unwanted marriage merely because she thought he might make a comfortable husband.

"Is there anything else I should know?" she asked brightly, hoping to change the subject.

"Ah, there is one more thing." For the first time, he appeared to actually read the words in the notebook, rather than just using it as some sort of shield. "I talked to Lord Reading about the blackmail case, you know."

"Oh, yes! Did he know who L. could be?"

Mr. Haworth shook his head. "He didn't have a name. But he suggested that L. might have been one of the men your brother knew from the Narcissus Club. Do you happen to know anything about it?"

Hester sucked in her breath. She knew a little bit about the club, but only because Simon had been a member. *Simon!* She expected her heart to ache at the thought of her former suitor, but, to her surprise, she felt nothing. Her heart must have healed over the last few months.

"The Narcissus club is patronized by the younger set in town," she explained. "It's very exclusive. I only know who a few of the members are."

He looked at her more keenly than before. "Do you happen to know if there are any members named Lawrence, or Lucas, or Lowell?"

She startled at the sound of Simon's surname.

Mr. Haworth didn't miss that movement. He leaned forward. "You *do* recognize one of those names?"

A shiver of cold dread swept from her head to her feet, but Hester nodded. "Colonel Lowell is a member of the Narcissus Club. Simon Lowell, I mean." She licked her lips nervously. "Do. . . do. . . you think Simon had something to do with the blackmail?"

"I couldn't say." Once again, Mr. Haworth evaded her gaze. "It's merely something to look into."

Should she tell him? Hester wavered for a moment, then took a leap of faith. "It's because of Colonel Lowell that I was sent away from London, you know. We were. . . we had been. . .

sweethearts, I suppose."

"Sweethearts" might not be a strong enough word. Her face burned as she remembered the embraces she and Simon had shared in dark corners, balconies, and gardens. She had been so certain that she and Simon would wed that she thought it wouldn't matter what they did together during their courtship. She was fortunate not to have gotten caught in something more compromising than a good-bye kiss.

"Oh. I am sorry to bring up such painful memories." Mr. Haworth darted his eyes up at her and grimaced. "It might not be him, you know. There could be more than one Lowell at the club."

"It could be him," Hester admitted. "I am sorry to say that Colonel Lowell seemed to be rather unprincipled." Though she hadn't admitted it to herself so bluntly before now.

Kissing Hester even after his marriage wasn't the first rakish thing Simon had done. One night, he'd cajoled her to walk down the dark walk at Vauxhall with him. She had resisted his appeals that time, thank goodness! For the first time, she realized that she would have been thoroughly ruined if she had followed him into the darkness.

"Well, it's something for us to look into, anyway," Mr. Haworth concluded. "But if you think of anyone with a similar name who might have a connection to the club, do let me know. Or let your brother know, though I suppose Frank has his hands full at the moment."

He rose to his feet and returned the little notebook to his pocket. "I had best return to the castle now."

Mr. Haworth hesitated, and she wondered if he was about to say something personal. This entire time, their previous conversation—the one when he'd more or less offered to marry her—had haunted her, lurking in the back of her mind while she tried to focus on other issues.

Was he going to say something about his near proposal? She sat up straight, hands neatly folded, hoping she looked like a perfect model of deportment. Whatever she might look like on the outside, internally, she fizzled like a shaken bottle of champagne. Her heart pounded, her hands sweated, and the very slight smile she forced on her lips felt shaky.

When the awkward silence lengthened, she tried prompting him. "Is there anything more you have to say to me, Mr. Haworth?" To Hester's relief, her cool, collected voice betrayed none of her inner agitation. For all he knew, she might receive declarations of love every day.

Walter Haworth merely adjusted his glasses and smiled a polite, emotionless smile. The moment Hester saw that artificial smile—so different from one of his real, engaging grins—she knew he had no intention of making any kind of romantic declaration. Her own smile vanished as if it had never existed.

"No, my lady, that is all. I wish you good day." He bowed, she inclined her head in response, and he strode out of the room, his long legs taking him quickly away from her.

She stared after him, surprised by how anti-climactic his departure felt. No, worse than anti-climactic. There were actual tears prickling at the corners of her eyes!

Hester had the sinking suspicion that she had, once again, made a fool of herself over a man who did not care tuppence for her.

Chapter Twenty-Two

"I SUPPOSE THIS has been rather a strange visit for you," Ivy said. She stood next to Walter as they watched the groom loading Walter's trunk onto the back of the travelling chariot.

Walter grinned down at her. "That might be an understatement."

Over the last three months, he'd dealt with embezzlement, blackmail, and underhanded scheming. He'd made the acquaintance of a marquis's daughter, a newborn cousin, and a ruthless scoundrel. He'd helped protect a damsel in distress, catch a criminal, and identify a possible blackmailer.

And he'd bruised his heart a little. Nothing that wouldn't heal quickly, though.

Lord Inglewhite stepped out through the open doors of the castle to join them. "I'll let you know when I hear about Lord Crowthorne's whereabouts, Walter."

The earl spoke softly, so that there'd be no danger of a servant overhearing. So far as Walter could tell, no one was supposed to know that Lord Inglewhite had any means of contacting Lord Crowthorne. For that matter, even Walter did not know how Lord Inglewhite meant to contact a man who had vanished after he reached America. But he did not need to know. That was clearly someone else's secret.

"Thank you, my Lord. And of course, if you should have any

need of me, you have only to drop me a line."

He shook hands with Inglewhite, bussed Ivy on the cheek, and climbed into the carriage. All that was left was a wave good-bye, and the pair of sturdy bays drew the carriage away from the castle.

Walter leaned back against the squabs and smiled as he discovered how well-padded the seat was. Though he'd refused to borrow the Marquis of Reading's carriage for the duration of a journey, Walter had not been allowed to refuse the assistance of Lord and Lady Inglewhite. Thus, he would make his journey home in the comfort of a plush, well-sprung traveling chariot rather than a cramped post chaise. He couldn't say he minded.

After a few moments, he pulled a journal out of his carpetbag and began to read about a cholera epidemic in India that had claimed the lives of a number of British soldiers. Medical experts debated how far the disease might spread, given that this outbreak was worse than previous ones.

Good thing there was no such thing as cholera in England! It sounded like a dreadful disease. Bodily functions did not normally make Walter squeamish, but the description of the "rice water purgings" stage was too much even for him. *Ugh!* He decided to skip ahead to the report about Dr. Parkinson's work on the shaking palsy.

Thanks to Inglewhite's assistance, Sir Henry Skelton had invited Walter to interview for the position at the children's hospital in a few months, once the plans for the charity were formalized. Walter knew his lack of a medical background would put him at a disadvantage, so he wanted to impress Skelton with his knowledge of recent advances in the field.

He dropped the periodical in surprise when the carriage came to an abrupt halt in front of the parish church. The coachman seemed to be talking to someone, although Walter could not see who. Rose or Frank, perhaps, running out to say a final farewell? He'd said his good-byes at the vicarage yesterday, but he would not mind repeating them.

But the face that peered in through the carriage window was neither his cousin's nor her husband's. It was Lady Hester Bracknell, looking as pale as ever, but not at all as composed as usual. In fact, she looked well-nigh distraught.

Walter opened the carriage door and leaned out. "Is something the matter, my lady?" His heart lurched as he remembered how easily young babies sickened. A cold that might be nothing to an adult could be deadly for a newborn. "Not something wrong with the baby, is there?"

"Oh! No! Alistair is fine." She stared at him, biting her lip. "May I have a word with you, sir?"

He frowned. "Of course. Would you care to take a turn about the garden? Or—would you rather sit in here?" Though it was the full height of summer, there was a cool breeze abroad this morning, and it might make a walk unpleasant.

She glanced back over her shoulder. "What I have to say won't take but a minute," she said. "It's only that. . . when I spoke with you yesterday, I had not realized that you were leaving today. I mean, I hadn't realized that it was our last chance to speak."

"Oh? Was there something you wanted to say?"

She lowered her eyes, and a delicate blush pinked her cheeks. "If you don't mind, I believe I shall sit with you for a moment after all."

"Of course." Before Walter could help her into the carriage, the groom was already assisting her. Then he politely stepped away, leaving them in relative privacy. "You seem unsettled, my lady. Is something amiss?"

Her thick, dark eyelashes fluttered. In another woman, he would have thought that a hint of coquetry. But she seemed genuinely embarrassed about this meeting. He could not imagine what on earth had brought her running out of the vicarage to flag down his carriage.

"Is there something you wish to say to me?" he gently asked. Something related to Butler's upcoming trial, perhaps? Or to her brother's blackmailer?

She gulped audibly, then whispered so softly that he had to lean closer to catch her words. "I cannot stop thinking about how I shall miss you."

Walter was stunned into speechlessness. His traitorous heart, though, pounded heavily. "I . . .I am honored." Was that really the best response he could give her?

She looked at him from underneath her lashes in that shy way that always made his heart flutter. "I was wondering, if I might be so bold as to ask. . . what do you think of me, Mr. Haworth?"

His jaw dropped. Proper young ladies did not ask questions like that. No matter how smitten they might be, young ladies were supposed to wait until a man declared his love, making his intentions clear, before they let out even a hint of their own feelings.

Had Lady Hester been waiting for Walter to declare himself? The idea seemed absurd, presumptuous, mind-boggling. But he could not imagine what else would have brought her here this morning. And even now, she was left waiting for an answer!

"The truth is that I admire you, and um. . ." Where on earth was he going with this? He had absolutely no idea what to say. What *did* people say in this situation? He ought to have asked for advice from Frank and Inglewhite. Both of them had managed to successfully propose to a woman.

For some reason, a phrase from *Pride and Prejudice* popped into his head. What was it Darcy said during his first proposal to Elizabeth? *You must allow me to tell you how ardently I admire and love you.* Well, that was no help. Walter couldn't make a speech like that.

He drew a deep breath, trying to steady himself. He was not romantic. He never had been. All he could give her was the honest truth.

"I think I might be in love with you," he blurted out. His face burned, and he knew he'd probably turned the color of a ripe strawberry. Nothing he could do about that but keep blundering on! "When I first met you, I thought you were—" cold and proud, he meant to say, but what a terrible way to begin a proposal of marriage!

Now that he thought about it, he might do better not to use Fitzwilliam Darcy as his model. Darcy had most certainly butchered his first proposal to Elizabeth.

"You thought I was what?" Lady Hester lifted her chin so that she could meet his gaze. He liked that she was tall enough that she did not have to tip her head far back to look him in the face.

Walter blundered on, though he suspected he was saying all the wrong things. "I thought you were very elegant and polished, but. . . as I observed you in my cousin's household over the last few months, I saw what lay underneath that veneer. I mean, I saw how warm and supportive you were when your sister-in-law had need of you, and how honorable and upright you were in all your dealings with those around you. I believe that I could love you deeply. That is, if you thought you could return those feelings."

Lady Hester blinked rapidly. "Then why didn't you say anything about it? Why didn't you declare yourself to me?"

A good question, Walter supposed. "I didn't think there was any chance you would accept a proposal of marriage from me," he admitted. "You see, I believed you were a distant star."

"A distant star?" She furrowed her brow in confusion.

This was why Walter preferred science to poetry! He was not good at figurative language. "I mean like a bright and beautiful light, far beyond my reach. Far *above* my reach," he clarified. "I did not think you would entertain the suit of. . . well, a solicitor whose family was only a generation removed from selling sugar. So, I decided not to ask."

She continued to stare at him, wide-eyed, waiting to hear more. He swallowed and forced himself to admit something else. "I suppose I was a coward, Lady Hester. I was afraid you would reject me, so I never gave you the opportunity. But"—a grin unexpectedly tugged at his mouth—"I will give you that opportunity now."

Lady Hester looked more confused than ever. "The opportunity to do what?"

His grin broadened. "To formally reject me, if you like. Now is your chance! I suggest you make the most of it."

The corners of her mouth quirked up in response. "But what if I don't want to reject you?" She spoke softly, but her eyes shone with an unidentifiable emotion.

"I would never be so ill-mannered as to demand a woman reject me if she did not want to do so. I mean, I wouldn't make her not marry me if she didn't want to not marry me." Sheer happiness made him giddy, and he knew that if he kept speaking, he would only utter more nonsense. "In such a case, I would probably have to kiss her, assuming that she didn't want to remain unkissed."

His lady love looked on the verge of laughter. "I'm afraid I've lost track of all the negatives in this conversation," she admitted. "I can only say that I *do* want to marry you. And I do want to be kissed. By you." She flushed that adorable shade of pink again.

"That," Walter said, "I believe I can help you with."

He leaned towards her, and she met him halfway. He'd meant to do no more than tenderly brush his lips against hers, but the sweet warmth of her mouth invited him to linger. She caught his lower lip and teased it a bit before breaking the kiss. She was almost certainly more experienced than Walter, which was probably for the best. He was so eager to learn that he bent his head down for a second kiss.

They might have kept kissing for an eternity if Rose had not popped her head out the vicarage door and shouted at them. "I say, Walter, what on earth are you doing out there? Did your carriage break down?"

Walter broke away from Lady Hester—no, from Hester, his betrothed—and laughed. "I think we are going to have some explaining to do," he warned her. Then he yelled up at the coachman: "I am afraid I will have to delay my journey, James. If you would kindly just drop me off here, then you may go back to the castle." His journey would have to be deferred, given how many things there'd be to discuss regarding the betrothal.

"But what shall I tell his Lordship?" James sounded well and truly shocked.

"Tell him there has been a change of plan," Hester suggested.

Walter and Hester clambered out of the carriage so they could go explain themselves to their family. It would, Walter supposed, be the first of many such explanations he'd have to make. And the worst of it was that Rose did not even attempt to look surprised! She merely smirked at them, as if she'd expected this all along.

For all he knew, Walter might be the only person *not* expecting this turn of events. But for once, he didn't mind the surprise.

Epilogue

April 1819

FOR THE LAST month, Lady Hester Haworth had scrutinized every piece of mail brought into Havisham Cottage, watching for a letter written on black-edged mourning paper. Her father had taken a turn for the worse, and she feared that the next letter from home would announce his demise.

But the letter that arrived for her from London today had been written on plain notepaper, not mourning paper. When she broke the seal to read her mother's message, she discovered that someone she knew had indeed died... but it was a death she could only briefly regret.

I am sure you still remember Colonel Lowell, her mother wrote, *given your dramatic encounter with him at the Duke of Creighton's ball last year, and the evidence that suggested he might have threatened C. It may grieve you to hear this, but I must inform you that he has passed away under the most scandalous circumstances. It seems he seduced Lord Grantford's wife, or so rumor said. In any case, Lord Grantford called him out. They met at dawn two days ago, and Lowell was shot. He died of his injuries a day later.*

I do not wish to rejoice over any man's death, but I must say that I am relieved to learn that our enemy is no more. I have already written C. to let him know it is safe to return to England. May I hope that you and

Walter will be there to greet him when he returns?

Hester stared at the paper. She half expected it to shake in her trembling hands, but it did not, because her hands did not tremble at all. A year ago, Simon's sudden death would have struck her as a catastrophe. Now, she found it difficult even to pity Simon, though of course no one deserved to die a lingering death from gunshot.

She had ceased loving Simon sometime during that incident in Ingleton last year. Perhaps that was the effect of coming to know Walter, and learning from his example how a real gentleman should comport himself. Or maybe she had seen enough resemblance between Simon Lowell and Neville Butler to realize that they were villains cut from the same cloth. She was well rid of them both!

Either way, she had already moved on from the pain of being jilted before she learned that Simon might also have blackmailed her brother. After that—well, even though they'd never found enough evidence to convict Simon, she had come close to hating him. She probably wasn't the only one, either. As Frank pointed out, a man who would blackmail one person might very well be blackmailing others.

No, she could not feel too sorry for Simon Lowell's death, especially since it meant that her brother could finally return to England. Lord willing, he might even be able to see Papa one last time. Joy bubbled up from her heart, putting an undoubtedly foolish smile on her face.

News this good could not wait until evening. She must hurry up the carriageway to the main building of the hospital, so she could tell her husband the good news. *Crowthorne was coming home at last!*

The End

Author's Note

Unlike many medical conditions recognized today, "migraine" has existed as a diagnosis for a very long time. Physicians in ancient Greece and Egypt described headaches that occurred only on one side. The Greek scholar Hippocrates (one of Walter's medical heroes!) described the visual auras that may precede migraines, while other medical experts in the ancient world noticed that migraines could be connected to women's menstrual cycles and frequently appeared after childbirth.

The English word "megrim" has been used to refer to one-sided headaches since the fifteenth century C.E. This was the original meaning of the word, and the *Oxford English Dictionary* documents the use of "megrim" in that sense throughout the nineteenth century. In this book, I have used "megrim" in its original sense, referring to Hester's migraine episodes. However, the word "megrim" quickly developed other possible meanings, so you may encounter other novels that use it to mean "low spirits" or "depression."

Today, "migraine" is understood to be a neurological condition that may or may not include a headache. Women are more likely to experience migraines than men, and migraine episodes can indeed be triggered by hormones, but the condition isn't limited to women.

In writing from Hester Bracknell's perspective, I've drawn on my own experience of migraines triggered by stress, hormones, sleep deprivation, and weather. My own migraine episodes are not usually as debilitating as Hester's, and I fortunately have a wider range of medications with which to treat pain, so her fictional experience differs significantly from my real-life ones. That said, one character's experience can never cover the entire range of symptoms a condition may cause, so readers who experience migraines may have very different symptoms than Hester. Any inaccuracies in depicting migraine or Regency-era medicine are my own.

About the Author

Anne Rollins is the pen name of an English professor who lives in Northern California with her family, too many cats, and an enormous collection of books. She has spent untold hours of her life rereading Georgette Heyer novels, and hopes that someday people will compulsively reread her novels, too!

Join me at the following:
annerollins.com
facebook.com/profile.php?id=100094523334798
instagram.com/annerollins23
threads.net/@annerollins23